Death
OF THE
Queen
OF
Hearts

Death
OF THE
Queen
OF
Hearts

Roman A. Clay

ARCHWAY
PUBLISHING

This is a work of fiction. Names, characters, places and incidents are the product of the author's imagination. Any resemblance to actual persons, living or dead, events, or locales is entirely coincidental.

Archway Publishing books may be ordered through booksellers or by contacting:

Archway Publishing
1663 Liberty Drive
Bloomington, IN 47403
www.archwaypublishing.com
1 (888) 242-5904

Because of the dynamic nature of the Internet, any web addresses or links contained in this book may have changed since publication and may no longer be valid. The views expressed in this work are solely those of the author and do not necessarily reflect the views of the publisher, and the publisher hereby disclaims any responsibility for them.

Any people depicted in stock imagery provided by Thinkstock are models, and such images are being used for illustrative purposes only. Certain stock imagery © Thinkstock.

ISBN: 978-1-4808-2313-6 (sc)
ISBN: 978-1-4808-2311-2 (hc)
ISBN: 978-1-4808-2312-9 (e)

Library of Congress Control Number: 2015918220

Print information available on the last page.

Archway Publishing rev. date: 11/17/2015

For my parents and D. F.

Chapter 1

The royal family had plans for Prince James's twenty-first birthday, but so did James, and they didn't include the royal family.

Everyone would be at the palace ball, everyone except his friends.

James went to his bedroom, tossed jeans, ball cap, and sunglasses into his bag, and headed to the garage. He nodded to his bodyguards, Rex Zook and Vern Farrell. They were parked beside James's VW Rabbit. As he pulled out, their uncertain looks amused James. They followed James's car closely.

James pulled up to the Ministry of Truth Bookshop, which his friend, Colin Smith-Courtenay, owned. Entering the empty bookstore, James ran down an aisle. As he glanced at his two bodyguards, they bolted from their car as though shot from a cannon. James exited to the back alley where Colin waited in his Mini Cooper.

James jumped in and howled, "Go! Go! Go!" As they skidded around the corner, he heard Rex yelling into his mouthpiece, "Hamlet's running!"

"I hope you have an elusive route in mind."

"Don't worry." Colin grinned. "They won't catch us." He shot into oncoming traffic and darted down an alley. He did a quick U-turn and parked behind two large dumpsters. Through the gap between them, they saw the bodyguards' vehicle streak past. Moments later, Colin pulled out and drove in the opposite direction.

"Silk, Colin. Very smooth."

Colin rifled through his bag for his flask. "A toast! To twenty-one, chum, and bottoms up." Colin took a long draw.

"Here's to no more birthdays!" James took a swig followed by another. "Let's jiggle some molecules, Colin."

Colin focused on the road as his arm fumbled around the back seat. He revealed a wrapped gift. "Happy birthday, James."

"This isn't from your bookstore?"

"No. It's something I bought. A book."

"You bought a book?" Laughing, the prince stripped off the wrapping, which revealed the title: "Princess Christina's Death: A New Investigation."

"Quite compelling stuff about your mother's accident four years ago."

A curtain of ice rose between them. "That's enough!"

"Terrific read. Eye-opening stuff."

James looked at the cover price and leafed through it. "You wasted your money. You shouldn't read this rubbish."

Colin reminded him, "You once instructed me, 'If you want to be my real friend, don't be another ass kisser. I'm surrounded by them. I want to be told the truth, even if it makes me uncomfortable.'"

"Yeah, well, I must have been drunk."

"Well, you're sober now."

"Yeah, but not for long." He flung the book out the window. "I owe you a drink. Let's get good and fucked up."

Chapter 2

When they entered the rented banquet hall, twenty of James's schoolmates erupted with cheers. When the doors closed behind James, confetti and balloons dropped from the ceiling. Deafening heavy-metal music blared, shaking the windows.

At the bar, James's friends lifted their rum glasses and called out, "Here's to James, twenty-one tonight!" They toasted again and again, the room spinning as James drank one double after another.

Colin interjected, "Slow down, James. We still have your presents."

"Then I'd better get to them, because this rum is calling my name."

James made it to the gift table and tore into the packages: a Rigby rifle, the finest audio headset, and a silver flask he pressed to his head as if answering a phone. "Hello? Sorry, I'm not here."

Everyone howled.

Colin gestured. "Come here, birthday boy. Here's my gift."

James saw a stunning woman in a Burberry trench coat. From her bare legs and high heel pumps, he gathered what this "gift" had in mind. Then she dropped her coat, revealing just a bikini bottom, her bare breasts full and nubile.

At one corner of the table, Colin set a chair and, with a swipe of his arm, brushed aside the remaining packages. Grinning, James took the seat. But glancing down, he noticed an envelope that had been hidden beneath the other presents. On the envelope was a single word.

Bunny.

Stunned, James lasered his focus on the envelope, even as the dancer circled her arms across his shoulders. She pressed her breasts into the back of his neck, but he ignored her. He opened the flap. Inside was a single sheet of paper with these words:

ST. LAURENT RESTAURANT RESERVATION
FOR MR. LAPIN.
TONIGHT, 11:30 P.M.

James looked around, suddenly very lucid. "Who sent this?" He held up the envelope to Colin.

Colin moved to the music, as the beautiful woman clung to James's neck. "Who knows?"

James shrugged away from the dancer. "Damn it. Who sent this?" He shook the envelope at his friend.

Colin stiffened. "Honestly, I don't know."

James stood and looked at his classmates. "Which of you bloody sent this?"

Each man pointed out his gift. The envelope had no giver. The dancer stood naked, waiting for her patron to return to his seat.

"Colin, give me your car keys."

"You can't be serious?"

"Please," James pleaded. "You've told me to seek the truth."

"Want me to go with you?"

"No, just keep her entertained." He turned to the dancer and kissed her with a passionate force.

James knew the reservation was for him. Lapin was French for bunny.

The St. Laurent was halfway across town.

James looked at his watch. He had twenty minutes.

Chapter 3

James assumed his mystery host must have wanted privacy because the St. Laurent had no nosy valet, just a self-serve parking lot with few customers. He pulled his ball cap down and his collar up. Inside the restaurant, he said to the hostess, "Reservation for Mr. Lapin."

She glanced at the prince and faltered. "Your Highness?"

James shook his head slightly then asked, "My table?"

She regained her composure and responded, "Right this way." She led him to a table for two in the back of the restaurant. Before the hostess left, he handed her a large bill. "No one knows I'm here."

"Of course, Mr. Lapin." She tucked the bill into her breast pocket and smiled.

Fifteen minutes ticked off. He waited because the person who sent him the note had written "Bunny," the pet name only his late mother, Princess Christina, knew and used.

James fidgeted and ordered a drink. He scrutinized each person as they approached his table, but everyone passed him by. The waiting slowly pulled him down into despair. Who would do this? And why? He sat nursing a double rum and a triple hangover. With his glass, he made interlocking wet circles on the polished tabletop. Then he saw a woman's face reflected in the table. He looked up expectantly.

"May we use this chair?"

"Don't be presumptuous."

As she turned about, the woman muttered, "Drunk."

By his third double, he assumed he'd missed the contact and rose to leave.

Then behind him, a man's voice whispered, "Sit down, and don't turn around."

James started to turn his head.

"I said, don't turn around. Or I'll leave."

James sat back down and waited. After a long pause, he asked, "Who are you?"

"I'm just a messenger."

"How do you know about 'Bunny'? Who told you about—"

"Under the table," interrupted the messenger.

James reached under his table, his hand moving in slow, expanding arcs. Two hardened lumps of chewing gum, one abandoned, the other orphaned. Then his fingers brushed a flat package taped there. He looked about then discreetly removed a clear, plastic sleeve. Inside was an unlabeled DVD. "All right, I got it. Now what?"

There was no response.

James slipped the disc into his coat. "Now what?"

Then he heard his bodyguard Vern's booming voice. "Okay Prince, you've gotten us in enough trouble. Let's go."

The other security man, Rex, came around the table and sneered, "Damn kid. I don't give a shit who you are. Our job is to watch you, and when you threaten that, it pisses me off."

James spun around. The messenger's table was empty.

Vern was more relaxed than Rex. "Blind date's over. Let's go."

"I have a car."

"You think we would let you drive alone?" Vern laughed. "We are done for the evening."

"But I have Colin's car."

Vern sighed and looked at Rex. "You drive that thing to the bookstore and trade places with the VW. I'll get the prince to the palace. If we hurry, we might salvage our jobs."

James kept the DVD close in the pocket of his coat. "It's nothing against you guys," he apologized. "I had plans Grandmother just didn't understand."

Vern admitted, "I know. I was twenty-one once. My parents begged me to celebrate with them and all my friends wanted me to go out with them."

"What did you do?"

He smiled. "I had a shitty night." He gave the prince a light shove. "But I'm sure yours was much more fun."

Chapter 4

Once in the car, James told his bodyguard, "I've got a splitting headache. Plus I'm exhausted. I'd like to go home."

"Sorry, that's not happening. We have orders to get you to the palace party, and we're following them."

James knew what the palace party would be: speeches, Mozart, and lots of pretty girls all groping for the glass slipper. Daughter of the duke of such-and-such. The sister of the earl of this-and-that. All smiles and capped teeth, all the perfect hair and millions in cosmetic surgery. With all the authenticity of plastic fruit.

And he knew, that they knew, that he knew, that everyone was actively currying favor for when he would become king.

"Take me home. Now!" James patted the DVD again, reassuring himself it was still there.

Once in his penthouse, James dismissed his butler. "I need absolute privacy until morning." James locked his bedroom door. He examined the DVD. Nothing was written on it. What could this DVD contain that required so much stealth? He placed it in his digital player and hit play.

Noise filled the screen.

Then an image of his mother appeared. Christina was wearing an elegant blue satin evening gown. She looked neither happy nor sad but ever so vibrant and alive. Tears ran down James's face as he heard her voice.

"Bunny dear, happy, happy birthday. But if you're seeing this, something dire must have happened to me. Listen, darling. You're the only one to tell my story. The true story. Because whatever they told you, whether it was a suicide, an overdose or an accident, don't believe them. It was murder. I have arranged for you to receive this when you turn twenty-one. Remember: trust no one. Remember me. Avenge me."

Looking down, Christina paused and sighed. Fighting the tears. "I will always be with you. I will always love you." She bit her lower lip as her image faded to black, then to a snowy noise.

He started it again, and when her face appeared, James froze the image and stared at the screen. His heart pounding, he trembled with disbelief and confusion. Sinking to his knees, he closed his eyes and put a hand to the screen. The lakes of pain instantly boiled away, replaced with something icy and full of cold fury.

"I swear I will uncover the truth. Nothing will stand in my way. Promise. I will avenge you."

Looking outside, the morning sky was a veil of crimson.

James had landed on a haunted shore inhabited by ghosts beckoning him to explore. But what might be waiting there filled him with despair.

Chapter 5

The glow in the eastern horizon brightened as the sun rose. As the morning light flooded the room, James watched as all the furniture cloaked in black, gray, and white gradually blazed into color.

Stretching his fingers, he remembered a dawn four years earlier when the morning light crept upon a knoll. It flickered into the dense forest that suddenly burst into flaming reds and luminous oranges.

Prince James looked at his hands and knew they would kill today.

"Stake out their trail, conceal yourself, and wait," instructed his grandfather, Prince Richard.

Waiting on the timbered crest, submerged in the deep growth, lay two men. They were both dressed in camouflaged suits, suits that were barely discernible to the eye but could not conceal their deadly intent.

Prince Richard whispered, "At dawn, deer leave their feeding area to sleep. Let them come to you." Richard shifted his body to find some comfort then pulled out a ChapStick and rubbed it on his baldpate.

Prince James, tense with apprehension, gripped his rifle. "I know, Grandfather."

"Always high ground, and always downwind. That's how you set an ambush!"

This would be Prince James's first kill, late for a seventeen year-old.

He wasn't eager to kill, but he knew his duty. His grandfather wasn't the sort of man who took no for an answer.

"Yes, Grandfather." James sighed as he listened to his grandfather preach.

"Pay attention! Don't underestimate your foe. On the battlefield, you'd be outflanked. Then you're dead."

But they weren't on the battlefield. They waited for a defenseless animal. "Yes, Grandfather. I understand."

Prince Richard did not acknowledge James's reply. Being consort to the queen, his duty was training the next generation of royals. But the queen's early reign was so burdened with other priorities that the education of their own son, Louis, had been neglected. Now Richard was making amends. Not looking for steel this time but for oak, Richard treated James as a sapling that needed straightening, pruning, and the tempering benefit of the occasional storm.

Stormy clouds drifted in, dulling the colors from some trees and draining it from the rest.

Then his grandfather raised his hand, a cautionary gesture of silence. He pointed down the ravine where something moved. Then from the dense cover, a single doe pushed into the clearing.

Prince Richard whispered, "Hello, lovely."

The doe was magnificent.

He nudged James. "You know what to do."

James's fingers felt moist. He lifted his rifle and squared the doe in the crosshairs of his sights. As he steadied his gun, a twig snapped beneath his elbow.

The doe stiffened, her ears pricked forward. She scanned the area before dipping her head to the grasses.

The doe's sleek beauty filled his scope. James concentrated on a patch of shoulder. This had to be done. He gave tension to the trigger and inhaled. His finger caressed then squeezed the trigger.

A jolting explosion echoed through the valley.

Unseen birds leapt as one into the sky.

As though untouched, the doe lunged forward, taking two

lightning leaps. Then the grace gone from her stride, a hitch, a jerk, as she crumpled into a heap.

James witnessed as she took a desperate final breath. Her last remnant of life, a perverse quiver of a hind leg.

Then stillness. It was over.

Richard stood and pulled James up with him. He bellowed, "Well done, boy!"

James couldn't take his eyes off his deed. The gunpowder tasted sour. Scraping and sliding down the hillside, he wondered where was his own quest to prove his worth in this fractured and confusing world.

As they approached the doe, his grandfather droned on about things James didn't particularly care to hear. He nodded when he had to.

Prince Richard was still a formidable man. Age and crankiness had put a stoop to his thick shoulders, but he stood a full six foot, two inches tall. The brown mane of youth had silvered on the sides of a shiny, freckled pate. His piercing blue eyes could easily belong to a man forty years his junior. He had the physique of a retired world-class rower who refused to go to fat.

James watched as the gamekeeper plunged a sharp blade into the nexus of shoulder and neck then toggled it about.

A crimson ribbon flowed from the wound, collected in a tarnished silver bowl that materialized out of a bag of royal treasures. Richard took the silver bowl and dipped two sharp fingers in the ruby fluid. He painted bloody slashes on James's cheeks and forehead while James tried not to flinch.

"You kept your head, made the decision, and shot straight."

The blood felt sticky as some trickled down his cheek.

James glanced at the inert heap on the ground, hoping the doe would resurrect and flee like play-acting games from his youth.

But this was no game.

Cradled in the old man's hands was something obloid and plum colored.

James's eyes widened as a chill stabbed through him. "Is that the heart?"

"To your first kill, James!" as the heart wobbled in James's cupped hands.

James stared at the organ, its blood seeping between his fingers and twisting down his wrists. At that moment, James realized this was his real test.

Richard grinned wickedly as he wiped a rusty smear of blood onto his pants. "It's tradition, son, a very ancient tradition! Now take possession." He mimicked taking a savage bite into the heart.

The teasing heart taunted his reluctant lips: warm, sticky, and smelling of copper, salt, and something wild.

With defeat and appeasement, he opened his mouth and pulled the heart right to his lips and ...

A woman's shriek shattered the moment. "What have you done?"

Startled, James fumbled the heart. It landed at his feet with a thump.

"Oh, God damn it," Richard snarled.

James's mother, Princess Christina, bolted out of the familiar bright-red Jaguar. Princess Christina, a striking woman, never more so when enraged. Her blonde hair, the color and silky texture of her son's. Even her off-white jogging suit and scuffed black trainers appeared haute couture.

"What have you two ...? James!" She noticed his bloodied face and rushed to his side. She gently brushed back his hair as though searching for an open wound. She turned to Richard and yelled, "You savage, what have you done to my son?"

"Christina, there's no sense in getting hysterical."

"Shut up!" She turned to James. "Are you okay darling?"

He nodded.

She glanced down. The heart nestled amid the riot of pine needles, broken twigs, and detritus. The striking contrast was so surreal only a brain buried in the dirt would appear more alien.

"My God, that's a heart."

"You stupid woman. Why can't you leave this alone?" Richard implored.

She noticed the doe on the leaves where the men had emptied the carcass. She turned to Prince Richard. "You bloodthirsty old monster." Devastated, her eyes burned, on the verge of tears. She exhaled and gathered composure. No time for tears now.

She spoke with measured calmness. "A doe. You shot a doe. That's against the law."

"Not on this estate."

"And what of her fawns, you old fool?" Ignoring him, she twisted back to James. "James, I'm so disappointed. I can't believe—"

"I shot the damn beast!" Richard shouted.

Like emerald lasers, his mother's eyes found her son's.

James quickly bowed his head and stared at the ground.

"Is that true? Is it?"

James raised his eyes, but he knew what he would see. His mother possessed that gift of all great actors—whatever feeling or thought was immediately shouted from every pore. He called it emotional transparency. The look he often saw was of love, affection, and encouragement. That real love was unselfish, involved sacrifice, and most of all, the truth.

In her youth, she admitted being obsessed with Bob Dylan's early songs. She believed listening to his lyrics couldn't help but be a good influence, and her favorite line was "To live outside the law, you must be honest."

The truth. That mattered more than anything else. That's what she wanted, and it blazed like a pure light within her.

James glanced at Grandfather and sensed cool betrayal and conspiracy in his eyes.

Richard blurted out, "I tell you I shot—"

"Stop, Grandfather. I shot the deer, Mum," James confessed.

Her proud eyes ringed with hurt. "You break my heart."

"He'll remember this when he becomes king."

She turned on Richard. "This is about instilling sangfroid in my son. This cold-bloodedness diminishes him, and I won't allow it."

"I disagree. Ruling requires certain sacrifices, certain reserves of character."

"For what purpose? Parades? An endless line of coffins?"

Richard picked lint from his jacket, unfazed by her remarks.

"Sending people off to war, leaving widows crying all over the—"

"Has your husband, Louis, ever cried to you?" interrupted Richard.

She scoffed, "Louis? No, never."

Self-satisfied he spread his arms. "Then I did my job."

"Your job?" Incredulous, she said, "I don't want my sons raised to become savages. I don't want emotional cripples."

"You seem to forget one thing, Christina," Richard reminded her. "They are your husband's sons as well. Let's not forget that. And let's not forget who he is." He moved closer to his grandson. "It was a clean shot, took her right down, no pistol death. You should be proud of him."

James could see his mother would not back down.

"No one," her eyes filled with cold voltage, "can ever take pride in this."

Chapter 6

James looked up at the walls of his penthouse and saw the mounted head of that first doe. In fact, the entire wall was crowded with his other mounted animal trophies.

High above the city, James had a view from the Squire Building, the single occupancy of the top floor. The penthouse had three bedrooms, a library, and a spacious living and dining area with all the amenities. It had its own private entryway with an elevator that required a key to reach his floor.

A gentle morning breeze animated the chandelier above him.

On hearing those sounds, James's mind reeled back to that last family meal with his mother.

With the palace chandelier gently tinkling a melody above his family, James took his position beside his younger brother, Malcolm, and opposite his mother and father, Princess Christina and Prince Louis. At one end his grandfather, Prince Richard, and the other his grandmother, the queen.

All eyes gravitated to James.

Malcolm nudged him and whispered, "They say when it's your kill it always tastes better."

"That's not funny." James gave his brother a stern look.

Woom, the boys' lifelong nanny, served each boy some venison.

Then a spoon slapped the side of a wine glass.

Everyone looked up as Prince Richard stood with his wine glass extended in salute. "Might I say, this fine meal is the property of our grandson, James!"

James's father stood, as did Malcolm. The queen raised her glass, and Woom nodded her approval.

Princess Christina caught her son's eye. He winced at her look of resentment.

"What are we toasting?" She interrupted the moment.

All the adult eyes pivoted toward Christina.

"Enough, dear." James's father tried to conciliate the parties.

"No! I will not stand by while you all cheer on barbarism." She turned her attention to Richard. "I don't believe people who support blood sports are fit to be parents."

James stared ahead, maintaining neutrality.

Richard lowered his glass and made eye contact with Christina. "What did you say?"

"Oh, I've made myself clear, Richard."

James spoke, "Mum, it's okay."

Richard snapped back, "You've said enough for one dinner."

"No, I haven't." As if toasting her own words, she held her glass out briefly and drank it down. "In fact, I've just started."

Prince Louis lacked the strength to stop his wife, but the queen did. She raised her finger and the room fell silent, as though she had omnipotent power. All eyes fell on her. With a regal tone, she said with firmness, "Boys, you are excused." She gestured to Woom.

Woom tapped the boys and escorted them out. As they left, the doors were drawn behind them.

James hesitated and told Woom, "Wait." He leaned into the door and listened.

The queen by habit tried diplomacy. "Christina, hunting is something this family has always done. Do you really wish to change all our traditions?"

"When something is wrong or unfair, change is healthy. Change is normal. Otherwise, we'd still be living in caves. If this family wants to remain relevant in the future—"

Woom pulled on his shoulder. "Enough, James. Allow your parents to speak in private."

James sighed. The battle would rage on and nothing would be resolved. He understood the differences his mother had toward tradition, toward life, toward royalty.

Malcolm agreed. "Yeah, let's go."

James held a hand up and heard his mother's final retort. "Hunting will only be fair when the deer have rifles."

Chapter 7

The solstice sun was blazing as James secreted the DVD away. He jumped in the shower and dressed. James stood taller than average and inherited his mother's facial features and lean, athletic body. From his father, a growing bald spot that James refused to disguise, keeping his hair closely cropped. *We should be who we are.*

He found his VW Rabbit in the basement garage. His detail sat in wait for him. He didn't care. They could follow him all they wanted.

Once seated in his car, James dialed a phone number.

"Yeah?" A groggy voice answered.

"Colin, we need to talk."

Colin said, "Okay, how about tomorrow?"

James started his car. "It is tomorrow."

"Okay, then how about tonight?"

"I'm on my way to you right now. Be there in fifteen minutes."

"Bloody hell."

"Get up. I need you to find something for me."

"Well, if it's that stripper I gave you, forget it. She danced for us last night then went on her way."

"I'm serious."

Colin's voice perked up. "Very well. Just don't mention our night to my wife. She's already angry about how late and how drunk I was. Not to mention I had to find a ride home."

James let him know. "Your car is at the bookshop."

"Well, that's good to know. Hey, tell you what. Meet me there."

"Gotcha."

James pulled out of the garage and winked to his detail that followed closely behind.

Driving alone, James headed onto the expressway. Looking ahead, he saw the approaching River Tunnel, but as the darkness embraced him, he realized he was no longer alone.

"Put your seatbelt on, Bunny."

James nodded as he clicked his seatbelt. He winked and smiled.

Sitting next to him, Princess Christina shook her head. "I guess nothing I've said makes any difference?"

"Mum, I remember everything you say."

"Then remember that every life is precious."

James looked at his mother. "But in order to live, something must die."

With the tunnel lights flickering across her face, Christina shook her head. "That's your grandfather speaking. He won't be happy until you're just like him." She stared back at him with conviction. "He loves celebrating death."

"Grandfather says every herd requires culling."

"He'd cull most of the world if he could."

"Why is everyone telling me what to do? What about defending myself?"

"Bunny, that's different. I just don't want you taking a life needlessly. Promise me, please." She stroked his hair.

He hesitated, knowing he would have to find a middle ground between his mother's beliefs and those of his father's family. While he loved her, he was not sure her pacifism was entirely defensible. In the end, he had to find his own way.

Changing the subject, he nodded. "You're the only one who calls me Bunny." He winked and smiled.

She grinned. "It will be our secret, Monsieur Lapin." Then a brief shadow of apprehension passed over her face. When they emerged into the sunshine, James saw the passenger seat was empty.

He was alone.

James pulled in front of Colin's bookstore and could see the closed sign swaying in the window.

The detail parked behind James. As he went past the security detail, Vern rolled his window down and asked, "We won't have to chase you today, will we?"

James promised, "Don't worry. I don't have another birthday till next year." He noticed Vern smiling, but Rex maintained a scowl.

Colin met him at the door. "This better be pretty damn important to bring me out of my beauty rest."

James chided him, "That would take at least six months."

"You look like I feel. Here." Colin held out an aspirin.

"Trust me, I feel like you feel too." He grabbed the aspirin and swallowed it dry.

"James, what's so important?" He locked the door behind them. Colin had sprays of freckles on his cheeks and neck. Topped by bright red hair that was sculpted into a blocky, three-inch crew cut. James thought it looked like someone's neglected hedge.

"You remember last night?"

Colin grinned. "Barely. But officer, I deny everything."

"Remember what you said yesterday on our drive?"

Colin plunked down into an old plush chair, a poster of Audrey Hepburn holding court over the nook protected by a fortress of books. It was their own private hideaway. "Refresh my memory."

James sat in an even older plush chair. The small coffee table between them was splashed with magazines. "About my mother."

"If I recall, you threw that conversation out the window."

"Well, I'd like to read it."

Colin rolled his eyes. "Well, well, well, a birthday epiphany!"

"Rum induced, no doubt."

"So why the change of heart? I thought you didn't read trash."

James gave a weak smile and less than transparent answer. "Well, only a fool never changes his mind."

Colin nodded. "Well, join the club. That book didn't have a wide distribution. In fact, I couldn't find another one if I wanted to." He stood and weaved his way around bookcases to the front counter.

"Do you know the difference between a bibliophile and a book collector?"

James shrugged.

"A bibliophile buys every book he likes. A book collector buys two."

Colin retrieved a second copy from beneath the counter. "Here. Happy birthday ... again. But if you lose this one, I'll be hard pressed to find another."

James patted his friend on the shoulder. "I'll cherish it." He read the cover: "Princess Christina's Death: A New Investigation." The book had been written by Anonymous. "Do you know who the author is?"

Colin shook his head.

James spoke pointedly. "Can you find out?"

Colin motioned for the book and scanned the front and back pages. "Well, the publisher isn't listed. Neither is the printer. Self-published," he sniffed. He thumbed through the pages and stopped at a series of photos, mostly of the accident. "But these photos credited 'Leon/Cyclops.' Yeah, I think we can. We just have to follow the trail and track down the author. You have the power to find this person."

James backed off. "I can't. Any investigation I do will draw attention from my family, and my mother said trust no one."

"Whoa. Your mother?"

"You didn't hear that."

"But I did!"

"Then forget you did."

Colin whispered, "Just tell me: is she still alive?"

James shook his head. "She spoke to me from the grave."

"Very well. Your secret is safe with me."

James leaned back and tipped a cup of tea to his lips. "Let's start digging."

"Well, let's be careful where we dig. We might find a septic tank."

"Okay, I'll give you twenty-four to find Anonymous."

Colin held up his hands. "Twenty-four hours? You're kidding right?"

"I need this."

"Well, at least I know how I'm spending my hangover." He motioned James to depart. "If you want this done, leave me alone."

"Fair enough. I need to do some reading." He turned. "Thanks, Colin," he said as waved the book. Then, like a furtive shoplifter, he concealed it down his pants.

Colin was the only one of James's friends he completely trusted. He thought, "If my hair was on fire, Colin would shove it in a bucket of water." His friendship was more rare and priceless than any book.

When he exited the shop, he nodded at his detail.

Vern had a relieved expression. James laughed. He would be giving them a break today. He just wanted to spend a quiet afternoon reading at the penthouse.

Chapter 8

When he made it to his penthouse, James made himself comfortable on his bed and started reading the suppositions of Anonymous. The night before and his lack of sleep brought the words heavy. Soon sand fell over his eyelids. Within a chapter or two, he drifted off to sleep.

When he woke, his butler, Warden stood over him, thumbing through the book.

"Give me that!"

"Sorry, James." He handed it back without hesitation.

"How much have you read?"

"Nothing." He bowed his head in apology.

Regardless, James knew he'd seen the title. "I wish to be left alone. Is that understood?"

"Yes, James. I have posted your public schedule, but I've also canceled today's engagements. I said you were feeling under the weather."

James was grateful. "Thank you."

Warden turned to leave but stopped before exiting James's room. "By the way, the queen has ordered Woom to come stay with us for a while."

James sat up. "What for?"

Warden kept his head bowed. "She feels Woom is stricter than I am and will not be duped as she claims I've been." He looked up as his face reddened. "I took a thrashing over your absence last night."

"But I don't want Woom here." All James could think of was the warning his mother had given.

"You will have to take that up with the queen."

"That I will."

A gentle knock echoed through the door and James spoke. "Enter."

Chapter 9

Princess Christina peeked in and asked, "Care for some company?"

James smiled and nodded.

She quietly closed the door behind her.

"Why the long face, Mum?" He had been his mother's counsel on matters big and small for as long as he could remember. It seemed an odd and uncomfortable position to be placed in. It wasn't until much later that he realized how isolated she had become and how poignant it was that despite her fame and popularity, he was one of the few people she could really trust.

Princess Christina smiled, but her passion faded. She looked distant in her gaze, lost in some world he thought he understood.

"Care to help with a puzzle?"

"I most certainly would. What do we have?"

James slid a tin box from atop his bed and opened the lid that pictured the Great Pyramids of Egypt. He turned it over and a thousand pieces spilled upon the parquet floor.

Christina lowered to her knees across from him. She tucked the hem of her dress beneath her. "Well, let's find the edges."

They worked to finish the outline when there was a knock on the door.

"Enter."

Mr. Saxby Colberg entered, holding a sheaf of papers. Immaculately dressed in black morning coat with black and white checked trousers. "Princess Christina, I was told you were here. I have some important papers for you to sign."

The properly dressed civil servant had served the Crown for over twenty-five years. Cadaverously thin, he moves with a stealthy grace. Sallow skinned, blue eyed with a tonsure of white hair, he often seemed to appear out of thin air, and no private communication was secure when he was around. Officially he was the second permanent undersecretary of agriculture. Unofficially he was the family fixer. The man who could make a drunk driving arrest or a sexual indiscretion disappear.

Christina insisted, "We won't need your assistance tonight, Saxby."

Colberg hesitated, his posture taken aback. "But Your Highness, these need to be signed tonight."

She stared up at him and answered more assertively, "You may retire."

As he departed, Christina whispered, "I bet you read lips and use telepathy, you little man in gray with ten ears."

James cocked his head. "Man in gray?"

"Don't you know how to read the men in gray?"

James shook his head, waiting for an answer.

She said, "All right, Your Highness, option A or option B?"

James smiled. "Option B."

"See how I controlled you?"

James shrugged. "But I chose. I decided."

His mother raised her eyebrows. "Really? What about options C, D, E, and F?"

"You didn't give me those."

"Exactly. If I control your options, I control your decision."

James pushed a puzzle piece into position.

"Remember a man makes his own options."

James snapped the piece into the interlocked outline. "I see ... I think."

Christina gained her son's attention. "People wear masks, darling. You must learn to read people; you must strike through the mask."

James dismissed her point. "I know, but perhaps I'll have a better mask."

His mother rattled her wrist and brought her watch into view. Without a word, she rose and turned toward the door.

"But Mum, we haven't finished the puzzle."

She looked over her shoulder. "Darling, we'll have to finish it later. I have some important issues to take care of."

James tried to delay her departure. "Your fame, Mum, what's it all about?"

She tittered, "My fame?" She turned and put her hands akimbo. "An accident, an illusion. When I married your father, I didn't realize that fame was a visitor who would never leave." She sighed.

"Is it worth it?"

"Why do you ask?"

James leaned back against the bed. "I watch you and Father. You're told where to go, what to say, where to sit, where to scratch, double quick. Your lives aren't your own."

His mother softened her expression. "There are many difficulties, but it's led to the best things that have ever happened to me: you, Malcolm, and your sister, Mary Frances." His mother lowered her eyes as thoughts of that deceased daughter bought back dark memories.

James wished Mary Frances had survived her birth. He would have loved having a baby sister. Looking at his mother, he knew there was nothing sadder for parents than burying one of their children.

Christina looked up. "Knowing you and Malcolm are there makes all the chattering, stalking, and insanity bearable." Christina pointed a finger. "Remember fame is a double-edged sword. Either it uses you or you use it … to make a difference." She winked.

James cast his lot. "I want to make a difference. I'm just not sure where."

His mother stepped toward her son so they were eye to eye. "What you must find is something you really care about, then put your whole soul into it. Remember, 'He not busy being born is busy dying.'"

James grinned. "Well, when I'm king, you will be my queen of hearts."

Christina hugged him with the strength of a mother. She scooted him around the bed and drew the covers down. "In you go."

He climbed in. As she tucked the blanket stiff to his chin, he apologized. "Sorry about today, about letting you down. Never again, Mum. I promise."

She smiled as she dropped the canopy over the bed. "No matter where I am, I am always with you." Her expression softened. "Improvise, darling. Improvise. I'll wake you and we'll see the morning light together."

He closed his eyes and listened to his mother depart from his room with the quietness of a rabbit. And like that she was gone. He was alone again.

On the floor lay the outline of the unfinished puzzle.

Chapter 10

James called out, "Mother! Mother! His forehead beading sweat, the darkness haunting his thoughts. James woke in a cold shiver, provoked by a nightmare barely within his grasp. He strained to capture its fragments before they dissolved. An SUV crashing, a bridge, screams, such a nightmare, such a dream of horror.

He sighed with relief; he lay comfortably in his bed. He patted life into his pillow and curled the blanket back over his shoulders. He dismissed it all and tried to drift back to sleep.

Just as his eyes closed, there was a knock followed by a creak of hinges as his door swung open. The light from the hall painted a silhouette of his father followed by Woom.

"Father?" He shook off the grogginess and squinted through the darkness.

Woom reached out for his hand. She gripped it with solace.

James asked with more urgency, "What is it? What's wrong?"

Louis stood over him. With shaken emotion, he stated, "James, it's your mother. There's been a terrible accident."

"What do you mean? Is Mum okay?"

"She has …" He cleared his throat, "She's been killed in a car accident."

James sat up and grabbed the chain of his bed lamp. "On a bridge?"

Louis stared at his son. "What do you know about a bridge?"

"I dreamt it. Was it on a bridge?"

"You got that from a dream? A dream?" Louis insisted.

"Yes, tonight!"

Louis looked at Woom and back at his son. "Yes, son, it was on the Old Boston Bridge. We don't know all the details yet, but we will find out more in the next few hours."

James looked at the nightstand clock. It was 3:30 a.m. "What was she doing out?"

Louis shook his head. "As I said, we will discover more in the next few hours."

James pulled his hand away from Woom and swung the blanket off. "We will discover more now." He pushed his way past his father as his butler entered.

"Where is my robe, Warden?"

Everything happened in slow motion, and not just the time but also in his family's actions.

"James, it's too early to do anything. We must wait for the police to do their investigation and then we will have answers." Louis had bloodshot eyes, his stress palpable.

James became agitated and turned to his father. "Then why wake me Father, if we can't do anything? She's my mum, I want to see her *now*."

"Very well, I agree. Let's go see her." Louis reached out and held his son close. "We have lost the most important woman in our lives."

James told the butler, "Warden, bring the car around. We are going to the hospital."

The queen made her way into the commotion. "Cancel that, Warden."

James turned to his grandmother. "If Warden doesn't take us now, I will call a cab. What do you think the papers will say if they see the royal husband and sons going by cab to see their mother? Do you want that?" James, all of seventeen years of age, stood toe to toe with his grandmother. James was resolute to choose his own option and to not give the queen options C, D, E, or F.

The queen relented. "Very well, we will all go."

"Of course we will," he said as he stared at the queen.

The queen held a finger up. "Watch the distance of your leash. You have reached its limit."

James dressed without showering, tossing on last night's clothes. They headed down the stairs. "Where's Malcolm?"

The queen cautioned James, "Malcolm doesn't know and isn't going to be woken up."

James nodded. Perhaps the queen was correct. "Very well."

The gates of the palace crawled with press, already alerted to Princess Christina's demise. The royal limousine roared past flashing bulbs as photographers swarmed like mosquitoes.

At the hospital, a team of doctors waited to meet the royals. They guided them past the throng of spectators, down a secluded hallway patrolled by police, where no one but the royals was allowed.

Shouts of "Can you give us a statement?" echoed from the crowd of reporters. A female voice called out, "More questions than answers, more answers than questions."

James and his father turned and looked for the face of that voice, but the flashing bulbs blinded their view. James called out, "Who said that?" only to be drowned by the din of screaming reporters. Louis coaxed James along, forcing him toward the morgue where his mother lay in wait.

Everything blurred together in a montage of disbelief.

Even with the demise of his cherished queen of hearts, James couldn't help but see the beauty in the body on the gurney. He wept for the one soul who always had his best interest at heart.

His father remained strong, taking in the sight of the deceased princess who looked as if tomorrow she would wake up and everything would be fine. But that was not to be.

Embittered, James accepted his feebleness. It was the short leash of power.

Chapter 11

Dignitaries came and went, all with notes of condolences. The scene oozed morose.

His grandmother and grandfather carried on as though business as usual. His father held a certain distance; the weight of grief hung over him.

A truncated sleep left James tired as the world buzzed over the death of Princess Christina. The media clamored for attention.

Remaining in his room, James sat on his bed, dreading the public funeral. An untouched tray of food sat on the side table.

Warden had finished arranging James's mourning clothes. "Would you like me to put this puzzle away?" He stood over the scattered pieces with only the puzzle's outline completed. It displayed the apex of the Great Pyramid, precisely as it was on the night his mother died.

James remained silent.

Warden kneeled down and was about to tidy it up.

"Stop!"

"You can't just leave it—"

"I want it framed exactly as is."

"Framed? But it's unfinished."

"Exactly. And so was mother."

"Very well, James." Warden bowed and left the puzzle undisturbed.

Chapter 12

James looked at his reflection in the framed unfinished puzzle of the Great Pyramid that James and his mother had left uncompleted four years ago. James wondered if he would have to finish it without her.

James closed Anonymous' book then rubbed his eyes. He hadn't noticed that late afternoon had come. A knock on the door. "Enter."

It was Warden bringing in a food tray. "No disturbances, please." Sitting up, he picked a roll but ignored it as he continued reading the book.

As James turned the pages of Anonymous' book, a stuck page released a small newspaper clipping. He turned it over and read the headline.

Woman Predicted Princess Christina's Fatal Crash

A photo of a woman, Colleen Cutter, identified as a psychic who predicted his mother's death.

James retrieved his phone. Entering Colin's numbers, he continued reading the article.

"Hello."

"Colin, have you made any headway?"

Colin sounded uncertain. "I'll get it for you. Promise."

"Are you standing close to your computer?"

"I'm right in front of it."

"Can you look up a Colleen Cutter?"

Within a few searches, his friend said, "She's a famous psychic."

"She also predicted my mother's death. You might want to tap her for info if you can't find the author."

"Well, you might want to tap her yourself. She's performing tonight."

"Where?"

"It says here at the Psychic Eye Theater on Cadsworth."

"What time does she perform?"

"Eight."

James noticed it was after five. "Right then. I guess I'll take this one."

"And I'll try to have your author by tomorrow."

"Good job. Let's catch up later tonight."

A soft tap on the door.

"Enter."

Warden came in.

"I'll be dining out tonight. Can you pull some clothes for me?"

"Right away, James." He moved toward the closet. "And where will you be dining, and with whom?"

"Alone, and I don't know where."

"Very well, James."

"When will Woom be arriving?"

Warden whispered, "She's here."

"Well, I see Grandmother wasted no time."

"She never does." Warden had the same look of angst across his face that James felt in his heart.

"Well, make the best of it." James carried the book with him to the bathroom. "I'll be ready in fifteen."

"So will your clothes, James."

"Thank you."

When James finished dressing, he removed a bolo from his hat rack and a trench coat.

Warden viewed him with a smirk. "Undercover tonight?"

"It's becoming a habit."

"So you plan on milling about in public, I take it?"

James nodded. "But I'm sure I'll be safe with Vern and Rex tagging along."

"With Vex and Rern, I'm sure."

When he made it to the garage he approached his bodyguards. "Boys, I'll be going to this place." He handed them a piece of paper with the address of the theater written on it."

Vern observed, "Cadsworth? The Psychic Eye? I know this place. Are you going to see Colleen?"

James took notice. "You know of her?"

"My mother is into psychic readings. She's viewed a show or three." He pointed to James's outfit. "I doubt you'll have to worry about your being noticed. The place is usually packed. The 'believers' are entranced with her. They don't pay any attention to what's around them.

"Well, I don't want to be a distraction until I need to be a distraction."

Rex grumbled, "I don't like the sound of that."

"Don't worry. Everything will be fine."

Rex pulled a toothpick from his mouth. "Somehow, nothing is ever fine when you are out stirring muck up."

Chapter 13

The security detail followed James as he parked his VW Rabbit near the Psychic Eye Theater. It was much larger venue than he'd anticipated.

As predicted James managed to sneak in without anyone taking notice of him. He found a spot in the back row of the packed auditorium. His detail stood by the aisle door.

Colleen Cutter entered the stage, bathed in a spotlight. She wore a robe, like an extra from a retelling of the three wise men. Her voice boomed over the crowd, "Psychotherapy is the ability to hold an object then tell its history." She held up her hand and shouted, "Does anyone have an object?"

Like kennel pups wrestling over a teat, the crowd raucously cheered and raised their hands. All the patrons longed to hear from loved ones "on the other side."

"You!" She pointed to a young woman midway up the rows of seats. "What is your name?"

Her assistant ran up the aisle and held a long thin microphone out for the woman to speak. "Clarice, ma'am."

"What item do you have?"

She withdrew an object from her pocket. "It's this broach, ma'am."

Her assistant snatched it from her hand and carried it high over his head so the audience could see no sleight of hand taking place.

When he made it to the base of the stage, Miss Cutter reached down and took it from her assistant. She held it out then rubbed it with her thumb. She closed her eyes, pulled it close, and stroked it against her cheek.

The crowd was silent in anticipation. James watched in fascination.

"Your sister, Corby, owned this broach."

The young woman in the audience gasped and clasped her hands to her face.

"She wants you to know that she misses you but you shouldn't worry. She says you may have the sapphire ring."

The young woman nodded as tears streamed over her cheeks. "Thank you. Thank you."

The crowd noise picked up. Each member waited their turn.

Colleen took another followed by another, guessing to the satisfaction of each eager patron with amazing accuracy. She called for her assistant, who escorted her down the stairs to the audience. She walked up the aisle, speaking to people in various sections. The crowd turned with her movement, all eyes fixed on this woman revealing the secrets of the dead.

When she neared James, his two guards stepped forward, but James ordered them back with a wave of his hand. James studied her as she uncovered a secret from a man only a few seats away. No one noticed the prince in the room.

James stayed for the entire show and when everyone filtered out, he ordered his detail to wait for him in the car.

Rex stared at him. "Is this your disappearing act?"

"Trust me, boys."

James slipped down a side hallway and found the dressing rooms. When he found her room, a security guard stood vigilant. "Sorry, no guests allowed."

James removed his hat and smiled.

"So sorry, Your Highness." He stepped aside and opened the door.

James entered and could hear someone humming a lullaby behind a curtain.

"Is that you, Marcus?"

"No, ma'am." James stood with his hat held in both hands in front of him.

"Without stepping from behind the curtain, she urged, "I'm not entertaining guests. Why did Marcus allow you in?"

"I have a question for you."

"No more questions. Buy a ticket for tomorrow's show."

"It's not that simple, ma'am." James remained calm and fixed in front of the curtain.

Annoyed, she poked her head out. Then stammered, "Prince James! Oh my, I do apologize. I didn't know, I really didn't know."

"I apologize, Ms. Cutter. I'm the intruder."

She came out, her hair pulled back with a towel wrapped around her head. She stripped the false eyelashes from her lids. She secured the sash of a ruby red robe around her waist. "How may I help you?"

James extended his hand and bowed. "Remarkable show."

Ms. Cutter fanned herself. "Thank you. I'm flattered you think so."

James escorted the psychic to a sofa and sat alongside her. "Can we chat for a bit?" James sensed her nervousness. "Please, just relax. I promise you I'm just as ordinary as you."

She laughed at the absurdity. "No, no, you are anything but ordinary."

"Nonetheless, I would like to speak to you."

"About?" She looked at the expression of unrest on James's face.

"About this." He gently reached for her hand and guided it to his wrist, laying it over his watch.

Her hand hesitated. Then she pulled it sharply away as if touching a candle's flame.

"What did you see?"

She paused and turned her head, unwilling to make eye contact. "It is from Princess Christina. A gift to you."

"And?"

"There's an engraving of 'To J, Love, Mother.'" She turned back around as a small tear raced down her face.

James removed the news article from his jacket. "And this?" James found it fascinating she didn't look but knew what it was.

"I had a strong feeling about your mother's death. A strong premonition that your mother would die violently."

James admitted, "So did I, but mine happened that night she died, while I slept. But yours is much more detailed."

She admitted, "I did something I've never done before. I went to the police."

James questioned, "You reported it?"

She nodded. "I did, but reporting a crime three days before it happened made me look daft."

"A crime? You saw it as a crime?"

Again Ms. Cutter nodded.

"Why did you think that?"

"I felt it. A snapshot. Something felt wrong."

James accepted this woman knew the nuances of her profession. "Is that all?"

Ms. Cutter stared into space. "No, there was something else. C.O. Debord."

James watched as she revealed her thoughts. "C.O. Debord."

He questioned her. "Who is C.O. Debord?"

Ms. Cutter shrugged. "No idea."

"Is there anything else you can tell me?"

She appeared drained, as though the psychic connection had stripped what energy she possessed. "Nothing."

James sighed. He wanted more. He stood up. "If there is anything else, can you please contact me at this number?" He handed her a card with Colin's number. "Much appreciation."

As he made his way to the door, she called out, "Wait. There is one thing besides the car crash."

James spun around. "Yes?"

"Do you remember her last words to you?"

"Of course."

Ms. Cutter smiled. "Beautiful sunrise … no, morning … morning light."

"Indeed."

She continued. "Be open to it. Morning light. It will impact your future."

James placed his hat upon his head and nodded adieu to her. "Morning light. I shall remember."

Chapter 14

When James approached his car, he saw a middle-aged couple chatting with Vern.

A sturdy woman wearing a coat over a red skirt and a faded blue blouse turned toward James and screamed, "Your Highness!" She pushed her way past the others and took a look at James. "My son, Vern, is in very special company."

Embarrassed, Vern stepped between them. "Your Highness, this is Mr. and Mrs. Farrell. My parents."

"Pleased to meet you, Mr. and Mrs. Farrell."

She attempted a poor rendition of a curtsy. "The pleasure is all mine. I hope my boy has been a good guard."

"He has been superb."

Mrs. Farrell continued. "I'm so sorry about what happened to your mum. Such a tragedy, and if you don't mind me saying, such a lovely woman."

"Thank you again, Mrs. Farrell."

"Oh please, call me Louise, Your Highness."

"Thank you, Louise."

Beside her was a burly middle-aged man who had a bum leg. His hip bounced as he limped unevenly. "Oh hell, my apologies, sir." He held his hand out. "Vern's dad."

James laughed. "Mr. Farrell. Please. I'm very fortunate to have your son looking out for my well-being."

"Well it's about time he did something noteworthy."

The air crackled with tension. The words of Vern's father had a bite to them. His mother briskly rubbed her son's back. "Vern has done lots of noteworthy things."

The evening had replaced the light, and an eerie layer of fog enveloped the area. An amber cone of light hung beneath all the street lamps; Rex leaned against the door, standing patrol like a sentry.

She looked at James's VW Rabbit. "Oh, such a nice car, Your Highness."

"Thank you, Louise."

She giggled.

James could see how overwhelmed his presence made her feel. "It was so nice to meet you."

"Oh, you're just saying that, but it's a lovely thought." She curtsied again.

Vern hugged his mother and gave her a final peck. "Take care, Mum."

James asked, "What does your father do?"

"He's an auto mechanic for high-end autos."

"Really?"

"Yes, he's a master at what he does. There is nothing he can't fix."

Then the three of them drove off. James punched it when he made it to the expressway.

Chapter 15

The detail saw him home, well past midnight. The evening had drained him. He made his way up the elevator. The dim light of a candle on the coffee table barely lit the front room. James passed Woom, who asked, "Did you have a pleasant evening?"

"I did, thank you."

"Where did you go?"

"Out."

Woom stood, a tiny woman, many years his father's senior. Two generations of princes she had raised. "I asked you where, and you say, 'Out.' Can you be more specific?"

James smiled. Having lived away from the palace had stripped from him the fear of Woom. "And that's all you're getting." He turned and continued down the hall to his room. "Have a nice evening, Woom." As he made it to the doors, he turned and reminded her, "And when you address me, it will be, Your Highness. Are we clear?"

With a Cheshire smile, she bowed her head. "Of course, Your Highness."

Chapter 16

James drove into a series of wicked switchbacks, flanked by greenery, leading to the three-story Bellefontaine mansion. Compelled, he floored the accelerator. He negotiated the curves as though his life depended on it.

When he arrived, he pounded on the ornate carved oak doors but received no answer. He kicked and punched it. "Let me in!" From the other side, he heard his mother and father fighting.

His mother bellowed, "Louis! You are a fucking liar." There in a second floor window his mother stood confronting someone. She cried and repeated, "Liar!"

His father opened the door and ran through James as though James was merely a ghost.

From the second-story window, his mother screamed, "Reptile!" as his father leapt into an Aston-Martin and sped off. Dust trailed his departure.

When James turned around, the window was empty and the house disappeared. Nothing remained, not even the car racing off.

His mother's voice called out, "Bunny, you've hibernated too long."

"Mum?" When he turned, instead of seeing her, he stood on a road with a speeding truck fast approaching. He couldn't move. The blinding lights in the dark of dreams brought panic. He shielded himself against the collision and then … woke in a pool of his own sweat.

From the other side of the door, Woom called out, "Your Highness, are you okay?"

He shook the fear from his consciousness. A dream. I'm fine. What did it mean? "I'm fine. Go back to bed." The green luminescence of triple digital fours gave him the time, too early to be awake. He stared at the ceiling, trying to make sense of it. He drifted back to sleep, and when he woke, the sun had brought in a new day.

His phone buzzed.

He answered a call from his father. "Woom said she heard you screaming last night. Are you all right?"

James admitted, "I'm fine, Father."

"I thought you were done with those."

"I was, until last night."

"Well, that concerns me. Since I don't see you much, and am saddled with so many preparations for my marriage, I need to make sure I have my teammates. You've been a little erratic lately. I understand it's your birthday weekend, but we need to focus on assignments."

"Those duties are … Father, something important has come up."

His father sighed. "What are you talking about?"

"It's imperative, imperative that we get to the bottom of what happened to Mother."

"James, that was four years ago. Everything has been investigated about what happened that night. There is nothing more to learn."

"Father, it's possible her death wasn't an accident."

James could sense his father's uneasiness. "Something's wrong. I can feel it."

"Feel it?" James recoiled from the thrust of his father's voice. "Is that how you make decisions … reach judgments? Feelings? It's inconsiderate to start this right now. Think of Gardenia."

James went silent, disappointed his father didn't have more faith in him.

Louis let out a breath and calmed. "Fine. Show me some solid evidence, some professional evidence, and I promise nothing will stand in our way of finding the truth. Deal?"

James echoed, "Deal."

Chapter 17

James made a quick round of interviews, mostly regarding Gardenia Morgan-Bowen and her upcoming marriage to his father. "What is she like?" "How do you get along with her?" "What's her favorite designer?" All questions he found utter nonsense but entertained for the sake of his royal family. The last question "Will you call her Mum?" elicited a response.

"Everyone has only one mum."

By nightfall he'd grown restless to find out more about his mother's death. He called on Colin. "Have we identified Anonymous yet?"

Colin chided him. "If you gave me something difficult, it would be done immediately but mission impossible, finding someone who doesn't want to be found takes a little time."

"Sorry, Chum. I will come by after I see an investigator tomorrow."

Colin's tone peppered with seriousness. "Investigator? Have you gone moon-mad over this?"

"I'll see you tomorrow." James disconnected and spent the rest of his night in his room doing an Internet search for private investigators, then rereading Anonymous' book from cover to cover.

Chapter 18

Morning came, and with very little sleep, he ordered Woom to bring him a strong helping of coffee.

James had found a private investigator in the heart of the city with a catchy slogan and opted give him a go.

His detail followed, and when he made it to his destination, he ordered them to wait in the car. He hurried into the Dorman Towers and checked the directory board. There at the end of the corridor, a glass door announced, "Brian Woods Investigations." This wasn't a prosaic gumshoe. He had a secretary, and his secretary had a secretary.

James sat in the outer room of a modern, high-class establishment waiting for someone to see him. His nobility didn't keep him waiting long.

A burley, pink-faced gentleman with an intense gaze came through an inner door and greeted him "Prince James. To what do I owe the honor of your visit?"

James nodded with no disrespect to his secretary and spoke softly to Mr. Woods. "May we speak in private?"

"Absolutely."

They reconvened in a more traditional office, books lined the shelves, and a general amount of disarray made this room seem more investigative.

"Sorry for the mess."

"No, it feels more the part."

"So how can I help you, Your Highness?"

"I'm looking for a discreet but persistent investigator." James continued. "Money is not an object."

"I didn't think it would be, but I must ask: what do you define as discreet?"

"You speak to no one but me."

"Agreed. What is your concern?"

"Well, I want you to find out what happened to my mother."

Woods leaned back in his chair. "Princess Christina's death? That's an unusual request. As I recall, your mother passed away in an accident."

"Perhaps, perhaps not. That's why I need discretion."

Woods's smile evaporated, "And if something did happen to her, why would discretion be needed? Do you suspect someone near to you?"

"No, but if someone did do something to her, they may have more power than the royal family."

"Very well. Is there a number where I can reach you?"

James kept hearing his mother's voice saying, "Don't trust anyone." He gave him Colin's cell number. No sooner had he made it back to the street, his phone rang from Colin's number.

"Hey, Col, what's up?"

"Did you just leave an investigator's office?"

"He called you already?"

"Yes, and please let me know that I'm not your secretary. Anyway, he said he's unable to take the case."

James couldn't believe it. That decision took less than five minutes. "What the bloody hell?" He sat in his car and went to another local investigator. This time it took even less time to be rejected. The offices of Wilks and Associates flat out told the prince, "To take on a case like this could put us in jeopardy."

James couldn't understand but lied, "I understand."

His third attempt found him in the office of Eric Blair. A smaller boutique firm, more in line with the investigators he'd watched in films. Blair, a bespectacled, bow-tied, tall man, tapped a pencil while the prince explained what he wanted.

"Well, that's an interesting request. You want me to open up an investigation that all the police reports said was an accident?"

"Yes, exactly."

Blair bobbed his head side to side as if weighing the pros and cons. "And what makes you believe it wasn't an accident?"

James sighed. "There are a lot of unanswered questions."

"Such as?"

James could see the wheels spinning in Blair's head. "I'll brief you if you take the case."

Blair smiled. "Normally, if I smelled fish from here, I'd kick you out, but since you are the prince of the country, I find myself intrigued." He nodded. "I would like to know what your objective is."

"It's my mother. I want the truth."

Blair winked. "Powerful medicine, the truth. There's a saying, 'The man who tells the truth gets run out of nine villages.'"

James held his resolve. "Then I'm on my twentieth village."

"And you're willing to pursue this no matter where it leads?"

That was the second time someone gave a cryptic response. "Of course."

Blair stood and clasped his hands behind his back and paced the floor.

James watched with anticipation. "Well?"

Blair studied the floor as if disturbed by some minor flaw. "All right, I'll do it."

"Excellent, I can brief you on what I know."

Blair held up his hands interrupting James. "Hold on. I said I would take the case, but I have a meeting I am scheduled for. Let's meet later this evening."

James felt disappointment. With reluctance he agreed. "Certainly."

"I realize you have a detail that follows you, and I assume they are to be trusted."

"No, I don't know who to trust."

"Sharp cookie." Blair whistled. "Well, that makes thing a little dicey. How about we meet at Beale and Green at, say, eightish?"

"Eight it is."

Chapter 19

James marveled at how easily he ditched his detail. Eluding them had never required such little cunning. That evening, they weren't at their designated spot when he entered the garage. When he left by the rear entry, they were nowhere to be seen.

He parked a block from Beale and walked to the corner where it intersected Green. James waited along the curb crowded with the tabloid boxes. He couldn't help but read a headline:

Prince James: Drunk or Drug Addict?

He snickered at the absurdity of the media exploitation and recognized the vast chasm between the truth and the news. As he read similar articles down the row, a woman crossing the street caught his attention. He could swear the woman was his mother. She had her figure, her hair, her nuance. He looked at his watch and decided to take a closer look. With a stream of cars clogging the street, he couldn't run it. He pressed the crosswalk button. Before the light changed, a car pulled up and blocked his view. His phone rang and he could see the number belonged to Prince Richard.

"Yes, Grandfather."

The car's window lowered, revealing Blair who gestured to the rear door.

James opened the door and was stunned.

There in the backseat sat his grandfather. "Get in, boy."

As he did, he glanced over the roof and no longer saw the woman across the street.

James felt betrayed. He clicked off his phone.

The ride took place in silence. James twisted around and noticed his detail followed behind. It had all been too easy by design. When they sped through the palace gate, guards saluted then closed the gate behind them.

James and his grandfather were followed by Blair. They met the queen and his father in the foyer. The queen dismissed Blair who bowed, and exited. James was certain that Blair received a handsome fee.

The four of them reconvened in the dining room.

"Tea, James?" The queen offered hospitality.

"No, thank you."

Louis spoke up. "Bravo, James, on finding such a good investigator." He waved a folder at his son. "But the information you seek is right here. I held off on telling you until we had definitive proof, but I can see you are impatient."

The queen leaned forward, as she took her seat at the head of the table. "All right, Louis, proceed."

Louis remained standing as James and Richard took seats. "The night she died, your mother had been at the Grand Hotel with Ali Hassan; that you know." He paused and looked for acceptance from James.

"Yes."

"But what you may not have known is your mother and Ali Hassan had been hounded by the paparazzi, suspicious of a possible affair." Louis scoffed at that. "So there they are, having dinner, along with Ali Hassan's father, Al Hassan. Meanwhile dozens of photographers were laying in wait outside the establishment. They were prisoners there that night. That's the reason your mother was out so late." He flipped a page and continued. "Cromwell Clay-Bauer, the head of Mr. Hassan's security team, had gone home because he wasn't feeling well. He took a prescription drug along with a few drinks. Then he returned to the hotel and failed to mention his mixing of drugs."

James could see that checkmate look in his father's eyes.

"So Christina and Ali depart, with every good intention of returning her home, accompanied with the two bodyguards, Clay-Bauer and one Clare Thornton-Smith. Unfortunately, Clay-Bauer elects to drive."

James's father moved closer, regret in his voice. "So you see, when the paparazzi start peppering them with flash bulbs, the impaired Clay-Bauer became disoriented. In order to escape them, he sped rapidly onto the Old Boston Bridge. Clay-Bauer, whose blood alcohol level was four times the legal limit, lost control on the bridge and crashed the car." He patted his son on the shoulder with fatherly warmth. "I'm sorry, James. Ali Hassan and Clay-Bauer were killed instantly. Christina made it as far as the hospital."

The queen put her hands together and nodded. "James, we are so sorry this was such a tragic accident."

Louis whispered, "There's a simple explanation. The paparazzi harassment made the driver take unnecessary risks." His father rubbed his forehead. "We lost her accidentally, James."

Richard chimed in, "Damn paparazzi should be shot, every last one of them."

James didn't reciprocate. "That's just the police summary. I've already read it from cover to cover."

His father lamented, "Yes, and when it comes to accidents, they're the professionals."

His grandmother stepped in. "I know it's difficult, but you must accept it was an unfortunate accident."

James stared ahead. "So accidental death is the only possible option?"

She stood and came to James. "Do you want it to be something more nefarious?"

James continued. "Eighty percent of the population don't believe it was an accident."

Louis plopped into a chair with an exhausted expression. "Everyone imagines conspiracies, but the truth is accidents do happen."

Richard frowned and softly offered, "Do you understand?"

James sat in silence, still not ready to give up.

The queen rested a hand on James's shoulder. "Do you understand, James?"

James lowered his head. "I do."

She turned her thoughts to another matter. "I know this sounds cold, but for the time being, we shall have no more of this and prepare for your father and Gardenia's wedding."

James felt sick.

Chapter 20

James remained at the palace overnight, after assuring his family he would bury his personal investigation. But in his heart, this was not over.

Early the next morning, he went to the stables, needing clarity for a life that felt diminished. The castle grounds were expansive and well guarded. Atop a horse for a solitary ride, mourning in seclusion could be achieved.

James waved off Neville, his stable hand who offered companionship on his ride. "No, thank you, Neville, I'll ride alone."

"Are you sure, Your Highness?"

James tightened a saddle strap and mounted his steed. "Quite sure." He leaned down to Neville, "No company, understand?"

"Yes, sir."

James booted a stirrup into the horse's belly and circled the beast to the rear exit. He slapped his crop; the horse bolted and the pair galloped into the morning dew.

James headed for the far end of the estate. He went there when he needed to be alone. It was there that a solitary Japanese maple stood sentry. Christina and he had planted the sapling when he was an infant. It became their tree.

Something kept echoing in his thoughts, the words of the errant voice at the hospital. "More questions than answers."

The metallic groan of a helicopter hovered high above him. He trotted his horse under the verdant canopy of the maple and brought him to rest. The branches could not muffle the sound from the intrusive craft. Its rotor banished the peaceful quiet in the solitude of nature.

James couldn't stay under the canopy forever. His steed chomped at the bit; his muscles twitched with anticipation. He brought the horse to the edge of the clearing as the helicopter spotted him. As it descended, James could see the flash of bulbs snapping in rapid succession. James kicked his horse and they galloped into the meadow.

The helicopter spun around as he passed underneath.

James could have easily eluded it, had he not seen something falling from the cockpit. The helicopter left as though spooked, and James could see why: a royal patrol helicopter approaching in the distance.

He circled around and headed for the fallen object. He dismounted and kicked through the knee-high field grass, which pelted his riding pants. He found the object, a red polo ball with a piece of paper bound to it.

A megaphone called out from the patrol helicopter. "Prince James, are you okay?"

James discreetly hid the note and waved the patrol off. He remounted his horse and read it.

We need to communicate. Tell no one.
Meet tomorrow at 1 p.m.
Courtland Art Institute Lecture on Nicolas Poussin:
The Hidden Meaning in Art: Et in Arcadia Ego

Is this meant for me? Maybe this is for Father. No, whoever took the photos had to know who they photographed and recognized me.

Malcolm startled James. "What are you doing?"

"Shit! Where did you come from?"

"I thought I'd fish."

James grinned. "Fish? You hate fishing."

Malcolm's face reminded James of their mother. He looked

drained of life. "I wanted to kill time." Malcolm tilted his head and gestured at the note. "What's that?"

James slid off the horse and approached his younger brother. "Don't tell anyone." He stood alongside Malcolm and held the note open to read.

"Who's it from?"

James shook his head. "I don't know."

"You think it might be about Mum?"

"That's what I'm going to find out."

Malcolm squinted and said, "Maybe you should give it to Grandfather."

James shoved his brother. "Maybe not!" James nodded. "And best we keep this between us."

Malcolm shrugged. "Suit yourself."

Pondering everything, James rolled the note over and over in his pocket. His father should see this, even though the mysterious intruder instructed to tell no one. He thought about it. Something convinced him this note wound up in the right hands.

Chapter 21

O n returning to the palace, James was intercepted by a footman. The servant intoned, "Excuse me, sir, but the queen would like your audience."

"Now?"

"Yes, sir."

James cast his arms aside and sighed, said, "Very well," and then followed the servant down the corridor to the queen's chamber.

The queen sat on a gold brocade divan surrounded by a number of red leather dispatch boxes overflowing with diplomatic correspondence and government reports. A hint of displeasure creased the queen's face but disappeared when James entered, replaced by a practiced warm smile.

"Come. Sit." She waved to a chair across from her. She motioned to the servant. "You may leave."

James wondered what she must have been like all those years ago before the weight of the crown fell upon her innocent head. She'd been at it forever, nearly fifty years on the throne.

She picked up one of her red leather boxes and sighed. "Ruling is like managing a sport team. One third of them love you, one third hate you, and one third are undecided. My job is to keep the third that is undecided away from the third that hates you."

"Why not join the third that's undecided with the third that loves you?"

The queen gave his impertinence a frozen look. Her reputation as an agile equestrian was displayed by her expert and effortless switch of horses.

She pushed a red box aside. "I'll deal with this later."

Amid the clutter, James realized every object in the palace had an invisible army polishing, cleaning, repairing, and when necessary, replacing. "You called for me?"

"I did." She put down a pen and focused on James. "It has come to my attention that you went for a ride today."

"It's a perfect day for a ride."

"Yes, but you went alone. You are very important. You are a generation away from the crown. You are far more important than you think. So wherever you are, you must not be alone. Agreed?"

Before he could respond, the queen chimed in, "Well, a morning ride. It's nice to see you returning to normal."

James found it hard to believe she had suggested normalcy since his mother's death. "Things will never return to normal."

The queen raised her eyebrows. "James, I understand your pain, but life must become status quo ante. Remember, we are the royal family."

Her strategy would not be to hammer James until he broke or, worse, rebelled but mold him until he had the strength to wear the crown and the confidence to rule.

"I expect you to make your own decision, and I expect it to be the right one." Meaning the same decision she would have made.

He was speechless at her audacity.

"I'll take your silence as acceptance."

A typical compromise for her. Whatever horse she rode, it always resulted in victory.

"Would you like lunch?"

"I'm not very hungry."

"Nonsense. A growing young man needs food. Food is the most important medicine."

"Very well, but something light, please."

"But we have venison."

James thought about his mother. "I'm not hungry for meat."

The queen viewed James with a queer look of disappointment. "Venison then."

James fought off the temptation to argue. Grandmother never accepted any other point of view besides her own. Arguing would lead to his callowness being tossed in his face.

Rather than eating, he maneuvered the food around his plate as the note played on his thoughts. For the first time, something other than his mother occupied his thoughts and the intrigue fascinated him. What could someone want to talk about? Did they know some dirty secrets of his family or the reason for his mother's midnight rendezvous? Maybe espionage or intrigue against the crown? Whatever the mystery, James wanted to be the one to uncover it.

Chapter 22

James had one crucial question. Things had been set in motion and he needed a confidant. Malcolm's age precluded much assistance and Woom watched James not for James's sake but for the queen's. His father, the one person he knew he could trust, had to be protected. His only possible ally who had the ability to help was Warden. But would he help?

That night as he prepared for bed, he called Warden in.

Warden entered James's room and asked, "You called for me, sir?"

James didn't like the address. "Since when have you called me sir?"

Warden stood to attention. "Since your birthday, sir."

"Well dump the sir, and please don't ever quit calling me James."

"Very well ... James."

James approached Warden and held a hand up in a gesture of silence. He closed the door. Coming up behind his butler, he whispered, "I need your help."

"My help? You always have it, James."

James hesitated. "Yes. But can I trust you to keep secrets, even if it might include keeping it from my family?"

Warden relaxed and let out a deep breath. "Only if your safety isn't in jeopardy."

James thought about the note. "I ... don't ... think mine is."

"And how would I play into this help?"

"I need to see someone in town."

"I gather this isn't your everyday meeting with a friend? Perhaps something more clandestine?"

"Perhaps."

"Do you care to elaborate?"

James considered what information required such stealth as dropping a note from the sky. "No, no, I wouldn't."

"Very well. But I will only agree if you allow me to accompany you."

James acquiesced. "You may accompany me to town then wait for me. My meeting must be alone."

Warden nodded. "As you wish." He turned to leave. "Is there anything else?"

James insisted, "Tell no one."

Warden opened the door and turned. Backing out, he whispered as he closed the door, "You have my word."

For the first time in a week, James slept without his mother's voice calling out a proclamation.

Chapter 23

To elude his security detail, James left by the emergency staircase and exited onto the street. Seeing Warden's car, he quickly entered and they drove off undetected.

Mother was right; this life could become a prison if you let it.

"Are you sure you don't wish for me to accompany you?" Warden asked one last time as they made it to the center of town.

"No, this must be done alone. Don't worry. Because of where it is, I suspect safety isn't something you should concerned about."

"How do you know that?"

"It's too public. Besides, when they dropped the note, that would have been the opportune time to have done me harm."

Warden shook his head. "I hope you are right."

James tossed on a ball cap and dark glasses and stepped out of the car. He leaned in and revealed, "I'll be in the auditorium for a lecture by Anthony Sharp on the Nicolas Poussin's painting Et in Arcadia Ego."

"Am I to assume you will be discussing the painting of four shepherds pensively gathered around a tomb in Arcadia, the imagined paradise?" Warden winked.

"How in the world do you know that?"

Warden confessed, "I've attended the lecture before."

"Well, I hope that makes it worthwhile."

Warden continued. "There's more to it than that. The tomb bears the Latin inscription 'Et in Arcadia ego,' which translates to 'And in Arcadia I …' but it is an anagram: 'I tego arcana dei,' which means, 'Be gone, I conceal the secrets of God.'"

James smiled. "Thank you, professor." He patted the car, uncertain that Warden's information was irrelevant.

James hurried in and positioned himself toward the rear of the auditorium.

On the illuminated stage were an empty lectern and the mounted Poussin painting.

James stayed hidden as interested patrons approached the painting. James sighed. Ten minutes passed. He checked his watch, impatient.

Then a dull, distant thud shivered the entire room.

A buzz of activity spun about the hall as whispers turned to chatter. A voice shrieked. Then someone raised his voice. "There's been an explosion in the street."

James caught the words. His first thought was Warden. He jumped from his seat and scrambled outside. Filling the concourse, people stood pressed against the glass, gawking at a car in flames. From his right, he saw Warden approaching him.

"James, we should go."

James held his ground. "I can't. This is important."

"Very well, but now you have me with you."

"Suit yourself." James eyed his watch again.

Thirty minutes went by as more people took up position in the concourse, more interested in the activity outside than a royal standing in their midst.

When they canceled the lecture, Warden reasoned, "I think your meeting will have to take place another day."

"I suspect you are right."

They returned to the car.

James had hoped to find out what secretive information had to be delivered in such an occult fashion.

James suspected the explosion that rocked the streets had spooked his mystery host who chose not to conduct the meeting.

Chapter 24

The following morning at the penthouse, James flipped through the TV channels then stopped at the news. He turned up the volume. The news had interrupted the diet of sports with a breaking bulletin. "Hannister was a photojournalist for the Review. He left behind a wife and two children and his death is considered a tragic accident blamed on his auto's faulty fuel line. Tragedy struck when a spark from a passing vehicle ignited an explosion."

Then on the screen were the most recent photos taken by the photojournalist, Hannister. They were of James riding his horse through the field the day before. Hannister was my contact?

James stared at the screen in silence.

Was Hannister just an unfortunate victim, or was he the target? Should I tell my father? It dawned on James the vast gap between TV news presentation and the deeper reality.

There was a knock on the door.

"Enter."

Warden entered. "Your father is here."

"Here? He saw the news?"

"Your father didn't need to see the news; someone brought the news to him."

"James!" From behind Warden, the voice of his father bounced off the cavernous hallway, the heels of his shoes clicking off a rhythm. "Why did you not tell me someone took photos of you yesterday?"

James eyed his father. Why had he not mentioned my trip? Did he not know that?

"It's much deeper than that, Father."

"What do you mean?" His father lowered his voice and took them out of earshot of any other members of the house. They settled in the library.

James pulled the note from his pocket and handed it to his father.

His father read the note. "Why didn't you give this to me? We might have found out something about your mother's death."

"I thought the authorities said it was an accident?"

"They did, but with yesterday's events, one wonders."

"Well, it wouldn't have mattered if you'd gone."

"Why?" Louis crossed his arms.

James confessed, "Because I was there, Father. Hannister never made it to me."

"You could have been killed." Louis read the note again and sighed. He stepped toward his son and put a hand on his shoulder. "James, I applaud your ingenuity, but that was unwise. Come to me with these things. I have a security detail that can stake out a place and keep me safe. And no further secrets."

"I'm so sorry, Father." James came to realize how foolish his move had been and he felt a surge of nerves shake his body.

Louis grabbed his son and hugged him. "I couldn't bear to lose another member of our family. Please promise me that you and I will look out for each other." He pulled his son away and stared into his eyes. "I know I've not been as good an ear as your mother, but I promise to work on it. And believe me when I say how much I admired the job she did with you boys."

James wondered how he would ever be able to replace her. "Thanks, but no one will ever be her. Just promise to be there for me."

"Of course. Always." His father crossed his arms. "Is there anything else about your trip? Did you see anyone you might have recognized?"

James recalled the people. "No, no one I can think of."

His father shifted his head and squinted. "Okay, if there is, let me know." The elder prince turned to leave.

"Father?"

Louis turned. "Yes?"

"Could the media have information on us that could get them killed?"

His father laughed. "Hardly. I welcome the media, and I am grateful the nation remembers your mother's death. I'm just worried they have information on someone else we should worry about."

"Like who?"

His father hesitated. "Let me do some research. I promise to keep you involved. After all, we are a team."

"Thank you, Father."

His father walked away with heels clicking as he went.

70

Chapter 25

There is a point where James stopped seeing his father as the omnipotent parent and instead as a man of mere human proportions: fragile and flawed.

Prince Louis seemed uncertain of his position. Despite being second in line to the throne, he was a man caught in the middle. Son of a queen and father to a future king, he seemed destined to be a mere footnote, a minor interregnum between two charismatic monarchs. And little that he did or said challenged that fate.

James knew that to understand a person he needed to know two things: what his dreams are, and what his fears are. With his father, they were the same thing: the throne. Louis was fixated about what the throne would do to enhance him rather than contemplating the things he would accomplish with it.

James assessed his father. Louis was balding with a weak chin beneath gentle eyes, but his lack of personal charisma made his future untenable. Wherever he stood, he was overshadowed by the queen, eclipsed by Christina, and eventually marginalized by his son.

James knew his father considered himself to be a serious man, a man of depth that the media overlooked and the world at large would never appreciate.

Chapter 26

"Warden, I am going to visit my mother."

"At the cemetery?"

"We'll be doing that shortly afterward. First, let's stop and get Mother some flowers."

Warden sighed. "Why do I suspect this is going to be an unpleasant trip?" He handed James the VW keys. "Are we ditching Rex and Vern?"

James had a steely resolve. "You know me too well."

"Just remember: better to know thy enemy."

James continued as they made it out to the front entry. "What's that supposed to mean?"

"Better to have something you are familiar with than a new detail."

"What makes you think we don't already?"

Warden questioned, "Excuse me?"

"What do you think Woom's job is?"

Warden defended her. "You don't know Woom as well as you think you do."

James grumbled, "I know her well enough."

They drove off in the VW Rabbit with Vern and Rex in close pursuit.

James made a call to Colin. "Meet me at the royal cemetery. Make sure you park on the street as far away as possible. Okay?"

They drove past the nearest floral shop, instead, finding one in the busiest part of town. When James stepped out of the car, the early morning army of foot traffic engulfed him.

Rex followed as though chained by an invisible umbilical cord.

James cocked his head and smiled. In a shout over the din of city noise, he stated, "You might as well come up alongside. I'm not doing anything fancy."

Rex caught up and warned James, "And you better not. I'm fed up with having to find you every day."

James pointed out, "Just remember whom you work for. If you think it's my grandmother, just remember I can have you removed just as easily."

Rex fired back, "Don't do me any favors."

James didn't much care for Rex. He held allegiance with the queen and didn't give a damn about the man he actually worked for. "Is that what you want?" James stopped outside the floral shop. "Because I'm sure I can arrange your transfer."

Rex stared straight ahead. "I take it we're here to get flowers for your mum's birthday?"

James softened his position. "Ah, you know my mother's birthday?"

Rex glanced at James. "Well, I'm sorry for your loss."

James stiffened. He liked Rex better when he didn't have to like him.

They entered the floral shop together, but a crowd of onlookers had taken notice of the prince and quietly gathered, peering through the window of the store.

James purchased all the roses, then ten bouquets of lilies, followed by ten bouquets of carnations. Then everything the store had in stock.

The female clerk behind the counter worked feverishly to tally totals as James kept piling on bouquets. She blurted in frustration, "Hold on, Your Highness. I'm having a time keeping up with you."

James withdrew a black credit card. "Just put three thousand euros on it and call it a day, okay?"

She held the card as though he presented her a gold brick. "Three thousand euros, Your Highness? I don't think the entire shop has more than two thousand."

"It doesn't matter. The only thing that matters is that my mother gets the attention she deserves." He turned to the gawking onlookers loitering the other side of the window.

By now, a crew of reporters had arrived and cameras worked overtime flashing with delight at a royal spotting. James waved his hand for everyone to enter. Shocked citizens pointed to themselves as if asking could he really be referring to them. James waved again and nodded while shouting, "All of you, get in here!"

Rex spoke into his ear microphone, "Vern, you better get in here."

As the wave of citizens poured into the small shop, James held up his hand for order. "How many of you drove today?"

Nearly everyone raised their hand.

"I have more flowers than I can possible carry. I would like the assistance of anyone who cared for my mother to join me in a graveside visit. Today would have been her birthday."

The clerk tried to interrupt over the tumult. "I can get them there."

James turned and winked. "No need. These citizens will do nicely."

She drooped her shoulders. "Since we're out of stock, may I come too?"

James smiled. "By all means. The more, the merrier. In fact, you can call the press."

She hesitated. "I don't think that's necessary. I believe they are already here."

James scanned the throng of at least fifty people who had pushed their way into the small establishment and another hundred congregated outside. Among them were several reporters.

One by one, James handed a bouquet to each person. When he reached the reporters, he asked each one, "Whom do you work for?"

Finally, one pudgy one said, "The Daily."

James asked, "How long have you worked for The Daily?"

The reporter hesitated. "Ten years."

"Did you know Hannister?"

"Hannister?"

"Yes. The journalist who died a few days ago."

"Quite well. We both were there the day your mum died."

"What's your name?"

"Leon. They call me Leon, Leon the Cyclops."

"You interested in an exclusive, Leon?"

Leon nodded once.

James handed him a bouquet. "Leon, stay close to me after we lay the flowers."

James finished supplying the crowd with flowers. He hushed the noise and asked, "All I request is that you give me two minutes with my mother before you lay your flowers. Just a brief moment where I can speak to her alone. Grant me this request, and I will be most appreciative."

The men all nodded their heads, and the women didn't have a dry eye.

James had won the crowd. Anything he'd ask would be granted.

As James led the procession out of the shop, he noticed the look of wonder on Warden's face.

The crowd dispersed, hurrying to cars to carry them to the royal cemetery.

James hopped in the VW Rabbit, and Warden questioned, "Am I to guess, this is your distraction?"

"Wait and see."

James turned the engine. They rumbled down the street and turned toward the royal cemetery.

As James pulled up to the gate of the cemetery, the first car along the road was Colin's. Colin stood speaking with a royal official, waiting for James.

James, followed by his security detail, parked in the royal parking area nearest the grave and allowed the commoners to take all the parking spaces. They clogged the entire lot, overflowing onto the roadside.

James made his way to Colin.

Colin asked, "I can barely see my car from here."

"It's perfect."

"What's the plan?"

"I promised my family my sleuthing is over. I can respect what they are going through with Father's wedding. So now we have to be really covert, because this is far from over."

Together with Warden, they waited for the onslaught of citizens to pour onto the royal cemetery. As they gathered at the entrance, James quelled the crowd. "Everyone, stay close. This is, after all, a private cemetery."

James's words had tightened the ranks of the crowd and Colin smiled. "I think I know where this is going."

James nodded to Leon, the reporter he'd spoken to earlier, and motioned him to come nearer. "Okay, Leon, stay close to me."

Everyone followed James to the gravesite; the detail watched James's every move. When James made it to his mother's tombstone, he turned and asked, "Can all of you step back and give me a private moment?"

A melancholy buzz ran through the citizens as they bowed their heads and stepped back.

James moved silently forward. "Option C, D, E, and F, Mum." Then he kneeled and whispered, "I'm sorry I didn't do this sooner. I'm so sorry. Father has tried, but his life is so busy he hasn't been able to get to the bottom of this. So now it's my turn. I'll make you and Dad proud, I promise." He considered the last four years, how he put the thought of her far back in his mind and allowed his unrestrained partying to overshadow her death. He placed a dozen red roses on her grave and withdrew one for the lapel of his coat.

"Everything I am and will be, I owe to you."

He glanced up and noticed Rex and Vern separated from the crowd, following his moves with hawkish concern. He looked over his shoulder and could see the citizens, waiting to move forward. He stood and slowly waved his hands for them to step forward. They engulfed James and moved around him as though water around a fish. James caught the arms of Leon and Colin. In the center of the crush of people, James took off his coat and exchanged coats with Colin. "Leon, you are coming with me." He pulled off Leon's hat and placed it upon his own head. He turned to Warden, who had never left his side. "Warden, sorry, but you'll have to deal with Vern and Rex."

"Very well, James."

James and Leon worked their way through the back of the crowd and stepped quietly toward the exit. The detail didn't realize it was James because he made it to Colin's car without pursuit.

Chapter 27

Leon asked, "What's the exclusive, Your Highness?"

"I have some questions for you. Get in." James unlocked Colin's car and they hopped in. He turned the vehicle around and darted away from the cemetery.

As they sped off, Leon asked, "So what do you want from me?"

James scanned the rearview mirror. With no one following, he slowed down. He glanced at Leon. "I want to know what happened that night."

"What night?"

"The night on the Old Boston Bridge."

"I don't know what you're talking about."

James sighed. "Look, no games. You said you were there earlier. Either you were lying then or you're lying now." James scowled. "I just want the truth. Otherwise, I will ask you to get out of the car … while it's moving!"

Leon had a troubled gaze. "It's complicated, Your Highness."

"Here is my issue. I've been told the death of my mother was an accident. If it was, why was your friend Hannister killed? And don't tell me his car explosion was an accident."

Leon craned his neck and checked behind them. He asked, "This is on the down low?"

"Of course."

"Then ask away."

"So start with the night my mother died."

"Okay. That night we were just doing our job. Your mother and Ali Hassan were fair game. You have to realize one good shot was worth big bucks."

"I get it. I don't like it, but I get it."

"Anyway, after they left the Grand Hotel, we all followed the SUV like dogs nipping at the heels of a mailman. They sped off and we sped after them, but we couldn't keep up; however, we kept going. It didn't take a rocket scientist to know something had happened. Everyone could hear the echo of a serious crash on the bridge."

"So what are you telling me? That you weren't the cause of the wreck?"

"Hell no, Your Highness. Sure, we showed up and took photos of the crash. I mean, sorry for the painful memories, but that was gold, pure gold. But there was no way we caused the crash."

James wanted to punch the pudgy photographer for his admission of joy, but he understood it was a job. "After the crash, how long did it take for you to get to the scene?"

Leon shrugged. "I'd guess a couple of minutes. Maybe more, maybe less."

James questioned, "Who was there before you?"

"No one. We were the first on the scene. Hannister jumped off his scooter while I took photos. He realized there were survivors and phoned it in. Then he looked around at the impact and took a couple of photos of the crash. He never took any shots of the victims." Leon bowed his head. "I did all those."

James stared at Leon.

"Your Highness, you may not realize this, but those pictures meant we had an exclusive. We all knew it meant boxcar bucks."

"I want to see every photo you took that night."

Leon grumbled, "Too late."

"What do you mean?"

"Someone bought them. Paid incredible money for them."

"Who?"

Leon looked bewildered. "Colberg, Saxby Colberg."

"Saxby Colberg? Are you sure?"

Leon nodded once.

"Colberg works for us. Are you telling me my family bought the photos?"

"All I know is Colberg purchased all my photos, negatives, chip included."

James squinted and prodded. "Come on, Leon. You mean to tell me you don't have a backup?"

"Well, if I did, it would be very expensive. Money talks, so I hope you're very verbose."

James slammed the brakes, sending Leon toward the windshield. James reached behind Leon's neck and held his head against the dashboard. "Don't fuck with me. I want those photos. As far as money, I will see to it that you are paid."

With his cheek driven hard into the dash, he whimpered, "I'm good with that."

James let go. He wanted to dislike Leon but conceded to him a certain mercenary charm.

"You know, I have a lot of Hannister's shots as well. I have never mentioned it to anyone. I doubt you'd want to see them though; there's nothing there. Shots of the car's exterior, the grill, and the bums of the victims."

"Bums?"

"You know, derrieres."

"Why?"

Leon rubbed his chin. "Well, not really their bums, but more their laps. He mentioned it was strange they didn't have seatbelts on."

"Would that have been worth killing Hannister for?"

"I don't know."

"I would like to see those snaps as well."

They drove to the city, to the flats over the central district, one-room dwellings for the terminally single class of people.

Once in Leon's apartment, Leon brought up the photos from that fateful night on his computer. Each photo was labeled with a time code and date in the lower left.

James had to give Leon credit. From the time the crowd gathered outside the hotel until the taillights of the SUV disappeared from view, he continued to click away, all while driving a scooter. James noticed the last shot of the SUV disappearing was stamped 12:20. The next photo in the series was of the crashed vehicle and stamped 12:25. He switched back and forth between the two. What happened in those five minutes?

Leon milled about his kitchen then shouted, "Would you like some tap water, Your Highness?"

James was too busy to answer. He scanned the crowd photo taken in front of the Grand Hotel. He scrutinized a fellow standing in the crowd. He enlarged the photo, focusing on the man's face. He yelled to Leon, "Do you have a printer hooked up?"

"Sure, just hit print. It will make a copy in my bedroom."

James started running copies of everything. "What about Hannister's photos?"

Leon came up behind the prince and pointed for James to minimize the photos. On the desktop, he indicted a folder called, "Dungeons and Dragons." "Click on that." Inside were several sub folders. "Click on the third one."

James read the folder's title: "Hannister's folly." He questioned, "A little paranoid?"

Leon looked incredulous. "Kidding, right? You've probably already ruined me. If I have to pay back what they paid me, I'm going to be ruined."

"Don't worry about that." The prince started printing every photo in the folder, photos of what looked like inconsequential shots.

"Not sure why you want snaps of empty seats."

"You never know. They might not be as empty as you think." James gathered the photos and stared at the shot of the man in the crowd outside the Grand Hotel. He knew that face and he knew he had to find that face. He collected the photos and removed a thousand euros from his wallet.

"A thousand euros? That's it?"

James shook his head. "That's all I have on me. I'll send you another thousand."

"Um, no offense, Your Highness, but what you are taking is worth twenty times more than that."

James closed the gap between them and pointed a finger. "Is that what you made the first go round?"

"I made fifty."

James scanned the sparsely decorated apartment. "I'm sure you have quite a cash cushion."

"So do I get more?"

"I'm not taking your photos, just these prints. How about ten and you can keep them?"

"What am I supposed to do with them? I'm not supposed to even have them."

"And yet you are selling them again?"

"Okay, I'll take ten. Cash."

James headed for the door. "I'll see you receive it." He tucked the photos into his shirt as he exited the building into a slight drizzle.

Chapter 28

James worked his way across town to Colin's bookstore. As he came around the corner, he saw his security detail waiting for him. He had to give Rex and Vern credit. They were becoming smarter about where James would eventually show up. He pulled up behind them and winked at Rex, who glared at him in his rearview mirror.

In front of them, Warden waited in the VW Rabbit. James put the car in park and stepped out. Neither Vern nor Rex moved. As he passed the car, he tapped on the window.

Vern lowered his. "Yes, sir?"

"I have to drop off the keys to Colin. I'll be right out."

Vern dryly said, "Much appreciated."

James traded Colin's keys for his coat. "How'd it go?"

"Rather well, considering."

"Considering?"

"Considering your boy, Rex, insisted I ride with them as he held me by the nape of the neck. I promised him you would return to the bookstore." Colin smiled and motioned toward the sheets James pulled from his shirt. "Did you get what you were looking for?"

"I did. Do you have something for me."

"Anonymous, he's pretty elusive. I still need more time."

"Very well." He gathered all his photos. "You have a manila for these?"

James made it back to the street and climbed into the Rabbit. "Let's go home."

Chapter 29

Mounted on the wall of his room, James looked at the framed photos of his mother in public, a few with her former body-guard, Kerry Bolles. Bolles had an imposing build, hard to miss in any setting. He held up Leon's zoomed image of the crowd in front of the Grand Hotel. He nodded his head. That is Bolles. But why? Bolles had been let go several months before her death. Why was he in that crowd that night?

James hurried to his door and unlocked it as he stepped out. He passed the hall filled with the animal trophies. Each mounted head no longer an impressive display of his prowess, but a shameful reminder of whom he had become. He passed a busy Woom preparing a meal inside the kitchen and followed the sound of the news playing on the telly.

Seeing a relaxing Warden touched James. The man spent his life at the beck and call of the royals. James felt sure these private moments were what he valued above all else. "Sorry to interrupt you, Warden."

Warden bounced to his feet and stiffened his posture. "Yes, James."

"Relax, Warden."

"How may I help you?"

"I need another favor. I need you to find someone for me. And keep it just between you and me."

Warden pointed out, "Isn't that always the case these days?"

"Follow me to my room."

The two men passed the kitchen, Woom turned and caught James's attention, but he continued without acknowledging her. At the door, James pulled out a key and unlocked the door.

"Locked?"

James didn't say a word, just locking the door once they made it inside.

"James, I must ask: what's wrong?"

"Warden, you work for the royal family."

"I work for you, James."

"Very well, but how beholden to my father and grandmother are you?"

"On paper, very. But if you are asking me if I would betray you, rest assure your secrets are my secrets."

James studied his servant, caught in a standoff, their eyes locking on each other. "I believe you. Do you remember Kerry Bolles?"

"Your mother's bodyguard?"

"I'm interested in locating him."

"Locate Kerry Bolles? I think I know where he is."

"How would you know where Mr. Bolles is? He hasn't worked for the family in over four years."

"Let's just say I'm friends with his barrister."

"Barrister?"

"It's a long story, but I can take you to him. But why not take this to your father?"

"Because I promised him I would not make waves during his wedding. I don't want to upset them and have them think I hate Gardenia, but I have to continue this. The truth needs to come out and if I find it, my family will be proud of me. I need your assurance that this will never leave your lips."

Warden steeled his gaze and slowly looked from one picture to the next. "I am the least of your worries. You have other problems, James."

"Woom?"

Warden shook that off with a wave of his hand. "She might be nosy and willing to buckle if asked questions, but she's easy to avoid. No, I am referring to your detail."

James sighed. "Believe me, I've considered that, but Grandmother isn't going to withdraw them."

"And how much longer will you try to cat and mouse them?"

James sat at his desk and put his hands to his face, rubbing the stress from his temples. "Maybe we shouldn't try." James looked up at Warden.

Warden was curious. "You wish to include them?"

"I don't want to include them, but if they know I'm investigating my mother's death, they will report my activities back to Grandmother. Perhaps if I ask them to keep it hushed, and if it still gets back to her, I'll have whittled down my suspicions to a few people."

Warden reminded him, "That includes me?"

James nodded. "Yes, it does, doesn't it?"

James was ready to start discovering what his mother wanted him to discover.

Chapter 30

When James and Warden made it to the garage the next morning, James pulled Vern and Rex aside.

"Morning, Vern. Morning, Rex."

Vern, the tall blond, nodded but kept his countenance on full alert.

"I was wondering how you got into this business."

His bodyguard kept as quiet as a palace guard at attention. "Sorry, Your Highness, we are not allowed to engage in personal conversations."

James informed him, "Excuse me, but I'm the prince, and you might be hired by the queen, but since we spend so much time together, it's time we chatted."

"Very well. What would you like to talk about?"

"What made you want to be in security?"

"You want to hear me say how I wanted this job because of my admiration for the royals?" He stood stiffly erect and spoke in a deep low voice. "Frankly, I find your family pompous."

James grinned. "So do I!"

He stared at James. "Present company included."

James shrugged. "Fair enough."

"At least you listen."

"You look like you played sports. Tennis? Polo? Maybe cricket or soccer?"

"I was a wrestler."

"You mean like grappling?"

Vern kept his vigilance. "Yes."

"What's that like?" James detected the ice thawing around his bodyguard.

"Well, back then it was great. Now I question some of my habits."

"Habits?"

"I wrestled all over the world. In secondary school, I was a star and wrestled year round. Won lots of championships, but I did some bad things to my body."

"Such as?"

"I wrestled at 178, but I normally weighed around two hundred, so I took a drug, Lasix, to strip my weight."

"Water pills?"

Vern smiled. "They were diuretics used by heart patients to shed water weight."

"Isn't that cheating?"

"I guess, but the truth is it makes you weaker, not stronger. The only redemption is that all the top wrestlers were doing the same thing, so no one had an advantage. We were all two hundred pound kids wrestling at 178."

"Well, I guess it all worked out well."

"No, not really. Now all the medals and trophies are meaningless and using the water pills led to dried up ligaments and chronic high cholesterol." He raised his brow to James. "In other words, stupid kids do stupid things."

"What about you, Rex?"

The dark-haired man whose muscled arms angled out from his torso revealed, "I played rugby, spent most my life in Australia. Now I like to read stuff like *Day of the Jackal*, *Tinker, Tailor, Soldier, Spy*, and *Honourable Schoolboy*. My wife gets them for me."

"Wife? How old are you?"

"Twenty-five."

"Sir, you are going to have to realize, the rest of the world doesn't have a platinum spoon. We're just guys who joined the force and were selected for this detail."

James felt shame. "My foot sandwich tastes pretty rank. Sorry. That was rude. So Rex, what makes a good security man?"

"You have to see everything but remember nothing. That's the art of it, to remember nothing." Rex looked at James. "Seems like you want ask us something."

"I'm going to help my mother's bodyguard. He's had a tough patch. I'd like you to keep this just amongst us, is that okay?" He traded glances between his two guards.

Rex grumbled, "Okay with me."

Vern shrugged. "Me too."

Then out of the blue, Rex whispered, "Remember intimidation is the key to surrender, James."

Chapter 31

James and Warden pulled up to the city jail, his detail behind them. "I'll be back shortly." James stepped out of the car and shouted at the detail, "Promise no tricks!"

They rested behind the VW Rabbit on the street.

James made it to a long hallway facing a series of barred doors. One door slid open and he passed into the next section as doors clanged shut behind him. Then the next door slid open.

He stepped into the visitor's room and found a bolted table beside two forlorn chairs placed against the battleship-gray wall.

A buzz from another door and a close-cropped inmate in blue overalls stepped inside.

"The Little Prince isn't so little anymore." A blackened-eyed Kerry Bolles nodded and paid enough respect to extend his hand.

James waved his arm for Kerry to take a chair.

Bolles squinted from his good eye. "To what do I owe the honor?"

"Mr. Bolles, I understand you're here for drunken driving, resisting arrest—"

"That's all?"

"And assault."

"Yes, Your Highness, I've sinned against the crown and accumulated a few demerits. But since my barrister is skilled in the legal arts, I'll be out within a fortnight. Contrite, repentant but reformed.

So my time is limited. I hope you aren't here to be my mental health counselor?"

James relaxed and crossed his arms. "Not exactly. I do have some questions."

"Don't we all. Perhaps your bodyguards aren't treating you well?"

"They're fine. I was more interested in you."

"In me?"

"You were my mother's bodyguard. Then you quit," James pulled out the zoomed photo. "Yet you were there the night she died. I'd like to know why?"

Bolles stiffened.

"What did you see?"

Bolles rapped on the table. "Guards! We are done here."

James tried to gain his attention. "Mr. Bolles, what are you afraid of?"

Bolles scowled then let out a guttural growl at James. "Do you really want to follow in her footsteps?" He rose and nodded to the jailer. "Take me back to my cell." As he made it to the door, he turned to James. "Let sleeping dogs lie."

A wasted trip. Bolles offered him nothing but mystery. James waited a moment then nodded to a jailor and left the way he came.

To his surprise, the street teemed with paparazzi. What the hell? Who tipped off my location to the press? He pushed through the first wave of cameramen and stared angrily at his detail, wondering why they allowed him to be swarmed.

He motioned Warden to move over. James was going to drive. As he pulled away with Rex and Vern on his tail, the paparazzi caught up and engulfed the Rabbit. They snapped shots like machineguns.

"How the hell did they know we were here, Warden?"

Warden suggested, "You have a detail that doesn't seem to be stopping this."

"Very well, hang on." The VW may not have been made for luxury, but the power under its hood could carry it along at a high rate of speed. James put distance between himself and the rest of the pack, including his detail. Ahead he saw a railroad train running on a parallel track and accelerated to catch the engine. It was pulling over fifty railroad cars.

As they raced to pull ahead of the train, Warden asked with a hint of panic in his voice, "What are you planning, Your Highness?"

"I thought I told you to never call me that."

"Well, right now I'm hoping for divine intervention."

James laughed. "Me too!" James saw a crossing gate with a clanging bell and knew this was a deadly race. He floored the accelerator. He pulled ahead of the locomotive by half a length. He calculated the risk then swerved across the tracks, shattering the crossing gate. They escaped a deadly encounter with the locomotive by mere feet. They left the rest of the cars stranded on the other side.

"Yes!"

Warden had a pasty glow about him. "I think I may need to find a restroom, James."

Their conversation was cut short by James's cell phone. "Hello?"

Colin said, "You are on the telly right now."

"Oh yeah?" James looked to the sky. A news helicopter hummed above them.

Colin changed the subject. "Come over. I have some news."

"Be there in fifteen minutes."

Chapter 32

James and Warden entered Colin's bookstore. "So this is the sanc-
tuary you retreat to?"

"Warden, you've never been in here?"

Warden politely smiled. "I've never been invited."

Colin came around an aisle of books and let out a surprised chirp.
"Wow! What's he doing in here?" He motioned at Warden.

"He's our newest partner."

Colin looked suspicious. "I guess if you trust him, I will too."

James asked, "So what's up?"

Colin looked at Warden once, then twice, raising his eyebrows
each time. He pulled James away and whispered, "Really? You
trust him?"

James echoed loudly, "Yes, I trust Warden."

"Very well. You want to go to a party tonight?"

"Party? Just ask Warden. It's been sort of a hectic day."

They looked at James's butler who nodded and asked, "Speaking
of which, I need to find a loo."

Colin grinned. "Right that way." He pointed to the rear of the
store.

James continued. "I'm not sure I'm ready to live it up."

Colin leaned against a bookshelf. "The party's at the Bartlett
Estate."

James sarcastically mused, "At Roger Bartlett's? You know we aren't the best of friends."

"You'll want to make this party."

"Why's that?"

"Anonymous will be there."

"Fantastic. What's his name?"

"I don't know his name."

"So is Bartlett going to introduce me to the mystery author?"

"He doesn't know him either."

"So how do I meet him?"

"Anonymous has a snake tattoo around his left wrist. According to my source, it will be obvious."

Warden caught the tail end of the conversation. "And what will you do with the detail, James?"

Colin whistled. "Well, I guess he is on our side."

"Warden, I don't see why they can't come and wait outside. After all, a vivacious party would be a pleasant distraction, don't you think? I'm sure if a butler told the queen that her grandson was going to tear up the night rather than work as a sleuth, she might welcome that?"

"James, I think you have pegged your grandmother pretty well. I will convey your change of heart."

Colin added, "Party starts at seven."

"I'll pick you up at six."

Chapter 33

Towering pillars, Renaissance paintings, chandeliers, and long tables groaning with hors d'oeuvres greeted James and Colin at the spacious Bartlett Estate. A large open bar beckoned the two to imbibe a drink.

James took his wristwatch off and handed it to Colin.

"What's this for?"

"Just hold onto it for me."

As they passed a crowd, all the women scribbled their names on pieces of paper and started coming James's way.

"A prince stag at a party. Now I know why Eliza told me to not catch any leftovers."

James graciously stored the names in his pocket as they moved away from the bar.

A voice boomed from behind them, "Well, look who is slumming!"

James swung around and politely offered, "Great to see you, Rog. You're looking very fit."

Soft around the middle, Roger Bartlett admitted, "You're lying, but I'll take it."

James asked, "Do you have the time?"

Roger sighed. "It's a sad day when a royal can't afford a watch." He stretched his left wrist out of his sleeve. "Half past." Roger's wrist bore no snake tattoo.

"Thanks, Rog."

Colin whispered, "Smooth."

Roger suggested, "This isn't your crowd. As I recalled at school, you didn't care for anything other than family and wild women. Just in the neighborhood and thought you would drop in? Or is Colin giving you a sense of pride in your people?"

James resisted Roger's bite. Much of their issues arose from James's cavalier attitude at the academy. "Broadening my mind. Do me a favor?"

"Of course, but I'm not loaning you a cent!"

James lowered his voice. "I don't really know anyone here."

Roger sarcastically asked, "Blonde or brunette?"

James added, "I was wondering if any writers are here?"

"Writing your life story and need someone with a grasp of English?"

Again James let it go.

Roger loosened his bite. "Writers? How would I know? I never read. Ghastly habit. Bunch of neurotic, lazy thieves, and those are the good ones."

James played along. "And the bad ones?"

"Bunch of reprobates."

"Well, be a good chap and introduce me to the more cerebral crowd." James smiled.

Colin whispered, "I better hang out here. No need to spook Anonymous."

James patted his friend on the shoulder. "Don't drink too much. I would hate to have Rex throttle you again."

"Good God, James. Would he do that?" Colin's face turned petrified.

"No, but they might be nice enough to drive us home if we get too lit up."

Colin waved James off. "No, thank you."

James followed Roger through the crowd. "Thanks, Roger. I know we aren't the best of friends. I really appreciate it."

"Well, you are the prince. I should show some sort of decorum. Besides, I might earn some brownie points from the ladies."

James sucked up. "I don't think you need me to gain the attention of the ladies."

Roger patted a gentleman approaching fifty on the shoulder. "Liam, have you written any books lately?"

A small titter of laughter broke out from a circle of four men. "Can't say as I have. I have written some checks."

"You all know the prince, I assume?"

Liam held his hand out. "Your Highness."

James cursed that men didn't shake with their left hands. He joined the circle and Roger excused himself.

"So does anyone have the time?" James followed each arm as they all raised to inspect watches. No tattoos.

He floated about the room, approaching gentlemen he suspected could be his elusive author. One by one, he eliminated them, either by waiting for that left wrist to reveal itself or with his trusty "Do you have the time?"

This might become cumbersome, if not a bit silly asking everyone for the time.

An hour went by and he quit resisting the hostess who kept offering him drinks from her tray. He suspected his mystery writer might not have shown up.

He took two drinks and carried them to a far corner where an elderly African gentleman dueled with a young, beautiful Asian woman in a game of chess. He downed his first Bourbon and Coke and nursed the other. On a whim, he asked the gentleman for the time. Without taking his eyes off the game, he lifted his wrist and held it out. Nothing. No watch and no tattoo.

"Thank you." James took a seat and sighed.

Neither player said a word. Then the woman turned in her seat and James noticed her t-shirt read, "I make boys cry."

She hunched over the board but maintained her conversation. "Sorry, I don't wear a watch either." She gently tugged at the sleeve of her shirt and exposed her left wrist. And there it was … a snake coiled around it.

James almost choked on his drink and thought, Anonymous. And he was a she.

She stretched her fingers and moved her queen. "Check."

The gentleman scanned the board and smiled. "You are not going to be beat by me." He softly tipped his king to the board and bowed his head. "I see I am beat in two moves and resign."

She smiled as he stood to take his leave. "Thank you, sir. You are a gentleman and worthy opponent." She reached out and tapped James on the shoulder. "Next?"

James slid over.

She continued. "Can you play?"

"I'm not bad."

"'Not bad' won't beat me. Great might."

James set his pieces in place and nodded for white to start.

The woman moved a queen's pawn forward.

James uttered, "Would that be a Torre Attack?"

She glanced at James. "Perhaps it's a Trompowsky or maybe a Stonewall."

James followed. "Or a London, a Richter, or Colle."

"Well, you do surprise me."

James countered with his queen's pawn. Ten moves later they had settled nothing, other than James's curiosity over Anonymous. He had a hard time concentrating and didn't move a piece for a few minutes.

"Your move, Your Highness, Prince James—"

James spit out, "Prince James George Louis Arthur Benjamin Albion. If we are formally introducing ourselves."

She bowed her head in acknowledgment. "Alba. Alba Song."

He followed the flow of her onyx hair that showered over her shoulders in flawless alignment. "It's very noisy."

"I beg your pardon."

James lifted the board. "Let's take this game elsewhere. Come. Follow me."

They found an alcove overlooking the guests who had discovered the outdoors. He moved a knight and repeated, "Prince James George Louis Arthur Benjamin Albion."

She moved a bishop and echoed, "Prince James George Louis Arthur Benjamin Albion." It caught in her throat. She frowned then laughed.

"Call me James."

She offered, "James," and tried it again, feigning difficulty. "James."

In their quiet isolation, he finally asked, "So Alba, I have a question. How long have you been Anonymous?"

Surprise was quickly replaced by a scowl. "If you're looking to serve slander papers, my publisher's lawyered up."

James held his hands up in surrender. "I'd just like to know why you wrote it."

She penetrated his stare. "Buddha said, 'There are three things that cannot be long hidden: the sun, the moon, and the truth.' All I did was toss a pebble in the lake. When people are told the truth, they'll do the right thing."

James considered his mother's words. "Perhaps." He hesitated. "Very compelling book ..." He moved his bishop.

She countered with her rook. "But?"

James looked up from the board and waited.

"Usually people compliment the book and then comes the inevitable but."

"But?"

"'But you're wrong' or 'But it's a lie.' People don't like it when you challenge the status quo."

James quipped with "But ..."

Even Alba couldn't conceal her curiosity.

"I couldn't put it down." He drew his other bishop to the center of the board.

"Very bold move."

"Some would say reckless," James conceded.

Alba countered with her own bishop.

"That's fearless, Alba."

"Some say impulsive." Stretching her fingers again.

James studied her. "Sure you want to do that?"

Alba comfortably nodded.

"Very well." He brought his queen out and took her bishop. As he released the queen, he saw the gambit she'd suckered him into. He found himself in checkmate. His distaste for losing didn't sit well, but he remained gracious. "You have me beat in two moves." He laid his king down. "Brilliant strategy."

"Some would say lucky."

"Some would be wrong."

A gentle fog rolled in from the west, and the temperature dipped slightly. They caught the hostess and retrieved two drinks.

Alba offered, "Would you like to ditch this party?"

James removed the straw and drained his glass. He cautioned her, "But we'll need to take your vehicle. I came with someone, and I have two bodyguards we must elude."

As she came up alongside him, he was caught by her height. She was taller than he first surmised. Maybe five feet, eight, svelte, and solid like a runner. "And you would like to conceal your whereabouts?"

"The press can be hounding, and not a real pleasant occasion. Believe me."

"Oh, I have no doubt about that."

James and Alba made their way to the bar and found Colin.

Colin's eyes widened as he said, "Did you give up on your quest when you found this beautiful woman?"

"Colin, meet Anonymous."

Colin scanned her legs and followed them up to her eyes. "Well, I'll be damned."

"Aren't we all?" Alba countered.

"Listen, I need to make a break."

Colin sighed. "Again?"

"Yep."

"And what do you want me to do?"

"Nothing. Just close the party down and when my detail comes snooping around, tell them you haven't seen me for a while."

Colin winced. "They're not going to buy that."

"I know. Thanks."

"Oh, what I do for you."

Then James and Alba found Roger in the bowels of the mansion, being the good host.

James interrupted, "Roger, quick favor."

Roger sized up Alba. "I'd say I've already done you a favor." Roger winked and excused himself from a circle of friends.

"We need an escape route."

"The front door isn't locked."

James smiled. "It isn't, but with the press hounding me, it might as well be."

Roger tilted his head, a curious glare. "Press?"

"They're here. You just don't know it."

"Yes, well, follow me." He led James and Alba down a long hallway. Behind a door, they descended a stairwell to a dark, musty cellar. "Father kept the wine cellar from the castle that sat on this site." He handed James a lighter. "This is all the light I have, but if you follow that stone tunnel," he said as he pointed to a dark chasm, "it will take you to the opposite side of the road. You will come up behind anyone spying on this party."

"Thanks, Rog, and I take back everything I ever said about you."

"Somehow, I doubt it, but I appreciate that. Now go. I need to get back to the party."

"How do we get out?"

"The door opens, but once you're out, you're out; it locks behind you."

James flicked on the lighter and they hurried into the tunnel. Shadows danced across the walls like phantom soldiers of ancient times. "A little spooky." James gathered Alba's elbow and she clung to his bicep.

When they made it to the tunnel's end, the door locked behind them as they exited. They hesitated in the night air and gathered their bearings. They stood far below the road opposite the estate, down near the last row of parked cars. They nudged their way up the ravine.

She whispered, "I'll get my car. Keep walking down that way and I will circle round. I'll meet you down by the entrance road."

James looked at the darkness ahead of him. "You can't be serious? There isn't a shred of light between here and the next dwelling."

She smiled. "You're a big boy. You'll find your way." She scurried up onto the road and disappeared.

James shook his head and walked away from the estate.

After a few minutes, suddenly a shaft of light lanced into the night then landed on his back. Looking behind, James saw a pair of headlights following him. He started walking faster but the car kept him trapped in its light. James started sprinting. He glanced back but the headlights kept coming … closer and closer.

James feinted to the right then headed up the rise. The car continued past him, got on to the main road, and drove away.

Bent over, hands on his knees and panting, James heard a car horn beep. He traversed the rise and saw an idling blue Prius. The door swung open and there sat Alba. "Hop in."

Once inside, James caught a waft of perfume. Apparently, this mystery author understood the charm of being a woman.

"Where to?"

James winced. "Can we hold up and talk at your place?"

She squinted. "Well, since you are the prince, I assume I'll be safe."

Chapter 34

Alba drove to the gentrified part of the city, modern rows of condominiums with store front ground floors. A young, hip-geoisie section of town.

As they pulled into a parking garage, James submitted, "You don't strike me as someone who would live in such pompous settings."

"Pompous? That's rich coming from you."

"Well, I mean, you strike me as someone who would live above a library or in the bowels of a houseboat on the river."

"Find me the houseboat and I will, but until then, this isn't so bad." She pulled into a numbered spot on the fifth floor and they walked across a small footbridge to the adjacent floor of the Merovingian Towers.

She led him to a modest one-bedroom apartment overlooking an enclosed shopping square. A fountain pulsed showers of water to a piano concerto.

She laid her purse and phone on the kitchen counter and tossed her coat across the couch.

"Beautiful view, Alba."

"Thank you." While James took in the scenery, she flipped on the kitchen lights and asked, "Wine?"

"Red if you have it."

"That's all I have."

He could hear the squeak of her twisting a screw into the cork.

Then the soft pop and liquid pouring. James turned around as she approached the living room with two glasses.

"Here, have a seat." She motioned to the couch.

James nodded and joined her. He accepted the glass and raised it in a toast. "To Anonymous."

Alba lifted the wine glass to her lips and her eyes widened over the brim as she nodded.

James confessed, "Time is crucial, so excuse my directness. I want to puzzle out what really happened to my mother that night on the Old Boston Bridge."

"Hmmm. You don't want any idle chitchat."

James held his wine glass with both hands and bowed his head, looking at the cushion between them. "Are you interested in working together?"

Alba tucked her foot beneath her and rested the other leg over her knee. She steadied her glass on her thigh and said, "Well, I'm …" She sighed. "I don't know." She weakly smiled. "Believe me, I'm flattered beyond belief, but …"

"But …?"

"But you really know nothing about me."

James nodded his head. "True." He set his glass on the table and held his hands open like a magician exposing nothing hidden. "Tell you what, show me what's in your purse."

Alba paused, tilting her head. "My purse?"

James nodded, "Just show me. It will tell me more about you than any words."

Alba retrieved her purse from the kitchen. She sat back down, occupying the cushion next to James. She opened the purse and pulled out its contents. First two medicine bottles and a pair of sunglasses. She gave each item its history. "Vicodin and Imitrex for my migraines." She waved the glasses. "Dark glasses when they don't work." She started a collection on the coffee table. She lifted out ChapStick and a glue stick. "Gotta be careful not to mix them up." She held out a pack of gum, "Glee gum with real sugar." Then a book.

"Appointment calendar with map." She continued to array her possessions on the table. She pulled out several cards. "Business cards." In her hand, several pens of various colors. A thick Swiss Army knife. "My go-anywhere tool." She handed James a pocket brochure. "List of safe fish to eat."

James studied it. "Good to have when you travel in a foreign country."

"Trust me, good to have anywhere." She continued with a silver coin. "My lucky Kennedy half-dollar, my wallet, three debit cards, and a photo of my parents."

James lifted the photo from the fan of things in her hands. He looked at her mother and father posed in front of an ancient stone temple. "Where are they?"

"Cambodia. Angor Wat, a Buddhist shrine."

"You are Buddhist?"

"I am. Aren't you?" She laughed.

James leaned over the table and excavated through the cross section of her life. "So here's what I know. You understand hardship but are a great planner." He held up the medicine bottles. "Plan A." He held up the sunglasses. "Plan B." He sifted through the items. "No makeup, no vanity, practical, healthy, lucky and close to your family."

Alba noted, "There's one more thing." She retrieved a semiautomatic pistol. "My Glock 19."

He lifted his glass and saluted. "Anonymous with a 9mm bite. Here's to strong convictions." James finished his drink.

Alba offered, "More?"

He held out his glass and she went to the kitchen, returning with the bottle.

"Thanks."

Alba pursued his offer. "You realize where this investigation might lead us?"

"Well, although I suspect you may be on to something, I can assure you the culprits aren't who you think they are. I suspect they are powerful enough to be a threat to my family." James handed back the photo of her parents. "Besides, if you made a promise to your parents, would you keep it no matter what?"

Alba refilled her purse with her belongings. "I understand, James." She sighed. "Working with you would put me in a spotlight I'd rather avoid ..." She paused.

"But?" James interjected.

Alba smiled. "But ... let's do it." She reached out and clanked her glass against his, tilted it to her lips, and slid the wine down. "But I have one rule. I always keep my professional and personal lives separate. No messy complications."

James pursed his lips and kept a stoic glare. Her beauty would be hard to resist. "No complications, agreed."

"So where do we start?"

James suggested, "With the only survivor of the crash."

Alba asked, "The ex-soldier?"

"Yes, the bodyguard, Clare Thornton-Smith."

"And where is she?"

"She is in a convalescent center. She's never fully recovered. Would you be free to take a trip with me tomorrow?"

She asked, "Will we have to evade your men again?"

James shook his head. "No, I'm going to tell them that you are working for me. That you are researching a new charity for me to sponsor."

She roared back, "Working for you?"

James raised his hands. "Just a ruse. We are partners. Believe me, I have no desire to try and tame you." He'd stepped into something he couldn't get himself out of. "I didn't mean that either."

"Just keep that up and you will find yourself without a partner." She poured another glass and winked.

"Fair enough."

They finished the bottle and James lifted his empty wrist. "Kricky, I forgot I gave my watch to Colin."

"Ah yes, your ruse to see everyone's wrist."

"Would it be too much to ask for a ride to my place?"

"The palace?"

James laughed. "No, I live in town."

"Will the search party be looking for you?"

James grinned. "No, they are used to my escapades and have come to accept that eventually I will return. Besides, they are too frightened of Grandmother to admit they have misplaced me." As if on cue his cell phone buzzed. He looked at the number. "It's Warden."

"Warden?"

"My butler."

Alba looked amused. "Oh."

James held up his finger to pause their conversation. Then connected his phone. "Warden?"

"James, the boys would like to know if you are safe."

"Like a painting in a museum."

Chapter 35

James woke the next day, refreshed. He felt a spirit within him, alive and percolating with zest. He shoved the sheets away and reached for his robe.

Warden entered and noticed. "James, you're looking radiant. Am I to assume you were with a young lady last night?"

"It was nothing like that. Purely professional."

Warden smiled but his eyes remained skeptical. "I see."

James laughed and leaned into his butler. "She's going to help me investigate Mother's death."

Warden's expression turned somber as he quickly turned and closed the door. "If you are correct and an outside force had something to do with it, you must be careful. Remember the reporter Hannister."

"Then you must be discrete."

Warden said, "I have a much easier assignment than you do." He cautioned James. "And remember it's not just you who needs to be careful. Your friend must be prudent as well."

"She's aware of that."

Warden shook his head. "Very well. What will you be doing today?"

"I start today."

"So soon?"

James reminded Warden, "Soon? It's been four years. I'd say I'm a bit tardy."

James showered and ate breakfast with Warden and Woom. He'd asked Alba to meet him outside his building, figuring the less anyone knew about her, the better.

Woom asked, "Where are you off to, sir?"

"An afternoon date."

"That's nice, sir. Where to?"

James smiled. "Not here." He politely gestured good day and walked to the elevator.

Warden waited with his overcoat and hat. "It may be windy today. Here is something to cover you." He fitted a fedora on James's head and brushed his hands across the coat as he buttoned a waist-high button.

James unfastened the button as quickly as Warden had fastened it and stopped Warden from doting over him. "Cease."

"I don't want your date to go bad." Then in sotto voce, he added, "And if I didn't do this, it would be apparent to Woom."

James smiled. "You're wise, Warden."

"Why thank you, James."

James pulled his phone from his pocket and called Alba. "Are you at the corner?"

"I am."

"I'll be down in five."

"See you then."

He disconnected and nodded to Warden. "Wish me luck."

"Godspeed is more like it."

"That too. How irritated are the boys?"

"They're fine."

"Do you think they will put two and two together if we go to see Thornton-Smith?"

"They won't, but you know they might report your whereabouts."

"Oh well. Nothing a good son wouldn't do, checking up on the well-being of the lone survivor."

"Very true, James. Makes you a good royal."

James left through the elevator and down to the garage. He tipped his hat to the detail and caught sight of Alba standing outside the garage on the street corner. She started to cross and he waved her off. He looked at the garage surveillance cameras and decided not to make her identity so easy to discover.

He pulled his VW Rabbit out of the garage with the detail behind him; he swung by the corner and Alba jumped in. Together they darted off down the street.

"I take it the car behind us is your security detail?"

Nodding, James checked his mirror.

They drove out into the countryside, through grass fields that a soft breeze undulated with gentleness.

"Where are we going?" Alba asked.

"It's called the Barrington, and it houses permanently disabled people who can't care for themselves."

"Is Thornton-Smith in that serious shape?"

James nodded.

They continued with the detail following close behind.

Driving atop a bluff, a regal manor stole the horizon. "The Barrington."

They pulled into a nearly empty parking lot. The detail lagged behind and parked with the engine idling.

"Let's go see her."

They exited and hurried against a chilly breeze.

Once inside they approached the front counter. James tapped a bell, the tintinnabulation dinged, stirring activity in the room behind the service area.

"Coming!" A plump little woman wearing scrubs appeared in an open doorway. "May I help you?" She did a double take on James. "Oh my, Your Highness. This is a surprise."

"Thank you, but I don't think I've had the privilege."

"Ms. Woolsey."

"Well, Ms. Woolsey, we've come to see Clare Thornton-Smith."

She smiled and tilted her head in confusion. "My, my, no visitors in months and then two in one weekend."

James stared at Alba who nodded her head.

"Right this way, Your Highness." She guided them to an elevator and accompanied them to the second floor. They ambled past a series of rooms, to a small gym with workout equipment. "You'll find her in here." She let them proceed ahead of her.

"Thank you."

There in the far corner, Clare Thornton-Smith, struggled to put one foot in front of the other with the assistance of a set of low parallel bars. An attractive young therapist coached her with encouragement. "That's it Clare, awesome job."

Ms. Woolsey interrupted and caught the attention of Clare. "Prince James is here to see you, Ms. Thornton-Smith."

Thornton-Smith looked up and the woman James remembered as being sturdy and robust had been whittled down to a broken fragment.

"What do you want?" Thornton-Smith struggled but managed to grin.

"Staying fit, Clare?"

Thornton-Smith leaned against a rail. "Ha! Remember when I taught you to ride? You tumbled off and hit your head."

James came up alongside and put a hand on Clare's shoulder. "Yeah, and I still have the scar as a memento."

"And you, miss?" Clare politely bowed her head.

"Alba." She held her hand out. "And you are the Clare James has spoken of."

"Yeah, I guess I am. Or I was." She turned her attention to the therapist. "I need to take a break. Why don't we meet back up in an hour?"

"Very well, Clare," responded the therapist as she and Ms. Woolsey stepped out of the gym together.

When they were alone, Clare admitted, "Well, I've been expecting this." She held on to James's shoulder and dragged her feet in spastic movements toward a table in the center of the room. "Miss Alba, could you be a darling and bring my walker?"

She brought it to the table as the three settled in. "Here you go, Ms. Thornton-Smith."

"Please, Miss Alba, call me Clare."

"I will gladly do so if you would please call me just Alba."

"Alba it is." She laughed.

James smiled, hearing Clare in good spirits.

"I'm sorry to dredge up the night you were injured, but I need to know exactly what happened that evening."

"I'm surprised it's taken you this long. I'll tell you what I remember, James."

Hoping this would bear fruit, James glanced at Alba, who had pulled a pad out and started jotting notes.

"I need your memory, Clare."

"Well, I think it's pretty well documented. You want me to recall it all again?"

"I mean, talk me through it. Start with the commotion outside the hotel that night."

Thornton-Smith sighed and studied the air, but her thoughts were far away. "Because of the paparazzi scrum, Ali Hassan had this idea that his security man, Cromwell Clay-Bauer, and I should be a diversion, a decoy, from them. I cited the first rule of protection detail work: 'Never separate the vehicles.'"

James grinned, thinking how his own detail hadn't learned that rule very well. "And?"

"So we didn't. A client traveling alone in a vehicle is totally unprotected." Clare hesitated. "So after a slight disagreement, we agreed traveling in one vehicle would be the best option, so Clay-Bauer drove."

"You let Clay-Bauer, who might have drunk too much, drive?"

Clare's face contorted. "Clay-Bauer? You have to be kidding me. He was sober as a teetotaler. Had I suspected even a smidgeon of a nip on him, he wouldn't have driven. That I guarantee."

Alba kept writing.

"Anyway, we hop in the SUV, your mum and Ali Hassan in the back, me in the front with Clay-Bauer driving. We dart out ahead of all the paparazzi and Clay-Bauer picks up the speed to separate us."

"Since they were on scooters, why didn't Clay-Bauer slow down? You must have shaken them in a mile?"

"Because we didn't shake all of them."

"I was told all the reporters were on scooters."

"Not all. One of them drove a powerful luxury car and another a little white sedan. Clay-Bauer was determined to shake them."

James asked, "So what did Clay-Bauer do?"

"Instead of taking the direct route, he drove down by the river because he knew he'd have more opportunities to shake the luxury sedan. We had a powerful SUV that could blow it away on the straightaway. But when we came to Old Boston Bridge, something didn't feel right. It was not well lit, like the main banks of lights were off. I turned to Ali and your mum and insisted they buckle up."

"But nobody did." James saw Clare become uneasy by the flood of memories. "And then what?"

"I don't recall. My memory is gone from that point on."

Alba handed James two photos and James relayed them to Clare. "Take a look at these."

Clare studied them as James came around the table. He bore down over Clare's shoulder and used a finger to point out a discrepancy. "This picture is at the hotel. Look at the right side of the SUV."

Clare shrugged. "It looks fine to me."

"Exactly, but look at the other photo." He helped Clare hold them side by side. "This one is after the accident. Look at the white paint marks on the right side." He looked at Clare. "Could that white sedan have hit you?"

"Your Highness, I just told you, I have no idea."

Alba interrupted, "Were there any other vehicles?"

"Alba, if there were, how would I know?"

James stared at Alba, his concern for the truth maddening his position.

James interjected, "The truth is all we seek. Nothing will happen to you, I promise."

A bead of sweat rolled off Clare's cheek. "Nothing will happen? I'm afraid if I remember ..." She closed her mouth and stared straight ahead.

James bent lower. "Remember what? Please, Clare, this is Mum we are talking about."

"You want the truth, talk to Al Hassan. Ask him why he sealed the inquest transcripts. Find out what he is hiding."

James's head snapped forward and Alba looked up from her pad. James had suspected Al Hassan. James could see the emotional moment had drained his mother's bodyguard. He patted her on the shoulder. "Thank you for everything, Clare. When you return to normal, you come see me."

Clare breathed heavily. "Normal? This is as normal as I'm going to get." She resigned and slumped in her chair, focusing on the random nicks on the table's surface.

As Alba and James made it to the hallway, James whispered, "I told you Ali's father, Al Hassan had something to do with this."

Alba replied, "Do you want me to locate where Mr. Hassan lives?"

"Trust me. My father has suspected he'd had something to do with the accident as well."

"But his only son was in the car. What sense would that make?"

"I can't answer that, but you heard Clare. Al Hassan is withholding secrets from us. We may have to roll over a stone that has a snake underneath it."

Chapter 36

O nce James and Alba returned to the parking lot, his detail scurried to their car, a scattering of nervousness. They knew the prince had no qualms about leaving them behind.

James and Alba drove into the center of downtown to Houghton's department store.

Alba asked, "You think he'll be at his department store rather than home?"

"I don't think going to his home is a smart idea. At least here we are out in the open. Besides, he's a hardworking man. I understand. Houghton's is more home than home."

James drove into the parking garage, his detail close behind. The Rabbit tore through the maze of twists and turns. The squeal of rubber on polished concrete. When they found a parking slot and walked by the security car, Vern lowered his window. "Are you shopping, Your Highness?"

James knew they certainly knew the proprietor of Houghton's. "Yes, a little retail therapy."

"Rex and I would feel better if we accompanied you."

James hesitated and thought about the direction this investigation had taken. "Join us."

Rex quickly parked, and as they exited, James could see Vern sliding a revolver into a holster beneath his left arm.

James nodded as his detail followed from a distance. Okay boys, if you ever earn your keep, make sure you earn it today.

Alba mentioned their piqued curiosity. "Your boys seem to be on DEFCON 1."

James placed his hand on her back and guided her to an escalator that led up a floor. When they reached the next level, they found an entrance to the department store and journeyed to the business offices in the rear.

At the office doors, a pile of newspapers and magazines littered the reception room.

Alba grinned and pointed. "Look, James, you've made the front page."

James glanced at the tabloid headline and read, "Prince James: Kidnap Target?" He nodded. "Don't believe anything you read." In the photo, James clutched a book with his face downward. "Not the worst likeness of me. I only look slightly deranged."

James directed Alba's attention to the reception room where they confronted a twenty-foot poster of Al Hassan accompanied by the words "You are Houghton's Valued Customers."

"That's a lot of person staring back at you," Alba observed.

They continued to a window where a slender young woman was trying to empty the chamber of a hole-punch. As they distracted her, the chamber burst open and an explosion of tiny dots of colored paper shot up into the air like a fireworks display.

"Damn," the young woman blurted. She glanced up at the James. "Oh my, Your Highness, I apologize." She looked around James at Alba, then at Rex and Vern who had taken seats in the reception area. "I take it you are all together?"

James turned and acknowledged his detail. "Yes, but just she and I would like to see Mr. Al Hassan."

"Do you have an appointment?"

James shook his head.

She frowned. "I'm very sorry. Mr. Al Hassan isn't taking visitors today."

James requested, "Is there any way I could meet him for five minutes?"

"Mr. Al Hassan isn't here. He's offsite at a meeting."

James sighed and pulled a card from his pocket. "Can you see that he receives this and that it's an urgent matter? I'd appreciate it."

"That I will, Your Highness." Smiling, she reached out and retrieved the card, stroking the outside of his hand.

James caught Alba's look of disgust. They turned to leave, and as they made it to the outer edge of the reception room, he couldn't help but notice the quickness to which the receptionist placed a call.

"Are you seeing what I'm seeing?" Alba interrupted his thoughts.

"You read my mind."

"Should we hang out?"

"No. If he wanted to see me, he would have told her to make us wait. This could get interesting."

The four of them made it back to the parking garage. Vern and Rex were as anxious as warriors before a battle. "Calm down, boys. I don't know why you would be worried about this place."

Neither man said a word.

James started the VW Rabbit and noticed Vern and Rex sitting in theirs, the engine quiet. James pulled up alongside and lowered his window. "Anything wrong?"

Nodding, Vern ordered James, "Someone tampered with our car. Go to the penthouse. Fast."

Alba asked, "Shouldn't you stick around, James?"

"They may be right. We need to get out now."

James pulled to the gate of the parking garage. Across the street, two men and two women huddled in conversation. When they saw James, their conversation ceased. Then one pair crossed the street and entered a car facing east. The other pair climbed into a car facing west.

James asked, "Did you see that?"

Alba smiled. "That the women were pretty?"

"True, but I mean that they are in parked cars facing in opposite directions."

Alba gazed at James. "So?"

"So whatever direction we go, the car faced in our direction will follow." He sat at the terminus after paying the token.

"So what do you want to do?"

"First, let's see if I'm right. If I am, you need to hop out and high-tail it."

"To where?"

"Here." He handed her a card with Colin's address. "Go there."

As he pulled out, one of the cars quickly tailed him, while the other car sped off in another direction.

Alba watched James's accurate prophecy. "How dare you give me an inferiority complex."

"I didn't think that was possible."

When they stopped at a busy intersection, Alba said, "I'll start on getting the inquest transcripts." She reached out and squeezed James's hand. "Be careful." Alba hopped out and blended into the crowd of foot traffic.

When the light turned green, James signaled left but turned right. The car behind also signaled left but turned right. James weaved in and out of traffic. When he had a chance, he darted down a side street. Before he could clear himself from the tiny road, an oncoming car blocked the street. He stopped, put his vehicle in reverse, and looked backward. But behind him, the first car had him pinned in. James held his arm out the window and raised his other arm to show he had no weapon.

Someone with a hood on and the gait of a woman exited the car in front of him. She didn't say a word, but she brandished a semiauto-matic pistol. With her free hand, she snapped a leaflet under James's windshield wiper and backed away from his car. Then as quickly as they had arrived, they darted off.

James sat in his car for a moment, collecting his nerves. With the street quiet, he reached out his window and dislodged the note. It read, "Stop what you are doing … Don't drive uninsured." He wanted to smile, but he realized he had been warned. He exhaled and picked up his phone. Dialing Alba, hearing her voice gave him peace. "Are you okay?"

"James, I'm at Colin's. You need to get here immediately."

"Are you okay?"

"I'm fine, but there are fire engines everywhere. The place is on fire."

"Shit." James rammed his car in gear and called Vern.

James asked, "What happened?"

"Our car was tampered with."

"Do you have it under control?"

"We are on the road again. Where are you?"

"Colin's bookstore is on fire. Meet me there."

Chapter 37

S moke billowed from the one-hundred-year-old brick structure, fronted by fire engines camped in haphazard angles. The police cordoned off the area with yellow tape.

James parked and hurried across the busy street and into a growing crowd of onlookers. Outside the bookstore, he saw Alba and weaved through the crowd, his face covered by his hat. As he pushed through the front line, an officer put his hand up. James lifted the brim of his hat.

"Your Highness! May I help you?"

"Let me through. This is a friend's store."

The officer turned to his superior who nodded.

James ducked under the tape. He came up behind Alba with an edge in his voice. "Where is Colin?"

Alba turned. "Don't worry. He's okay. Something about an electrical fire."

"Electrical my ass. I've just got warned."

"Warned? Did something happen?"

James nodded. "Yeah. Subtle as an ax head." He stepped toward the building as the smoke tapered down, the smell of thick soot and wet piles of debris. Most of Colin's books were unrecognizable, transformed into costly fuel logs. Alba followed him.

Colin came around the corner, his face blackened, his clothes showing the wear of someone who fought in vain to save his store. He had a distant, defeated gaze.

"Colin, you okay?" James met him halfway and put his hand on his slumped shoulder.

"It's … everything … gone." His eyes red from smoke and tears. "What am I going to do?"

"Don't worry. You're safe. I'll take care of this."

"That's not the point, James. I built this, me. I didn't need anyone's help."

"Well," James said as he smiled. "Just accept my help."

"I should have known that wiring would falter someday."

James questioned, "What makes you think it was faulty wiring?"

"The captain of the fire department brought out the power box and said so."

"Come here." James poked his head through a gaping hole where the front window had welcomed readers from across the city. He studied the burned wood. "Look at this."

Colin and Alba followed James's hand as he traced the marks on the burned wood.

James whispered, "Keep this to ourselves, but that's an accelerant burn. This fire didn't start from faulty wiring; it was set."

Colin exchanged glances at James and Alba. "Then this was a warning."

James turned and winced. He needed to report this to his father. He looked around for Vern and Rex, but they were nowhere to be seen. All he saw were onlookers.

Voices from the crowd shouted, "Prince James? Why are you here? Who do you know here?"

"Alba, we need to leave." He scanned the crowd again, reached in his pocket, and pulled out his phone. He served up the number for Vern but it went to voicemail. "Odd."

Colin asked, "Who are you trying to reach?"

"My detail."

Alba asked, "Don't they always answer?"

James said in disgust, "Always."

Colin stood, defeated shoulders and tired eyes, but managed a small grin. "I always wondered if something like this happened and I could only save one book, which one would it be." Colin shrugged sadly.

"And don't worry about the store. We'll fix this."

Chapter 38

James had escorted Alba back to her apartment.

When he returned to his VW, two cars skidded to a stop, pinning it against the curb. His hands nestled into his trench coat pockets. He remained calm as two men stepped out of the rear car, both well dressed but clearly in earnest. One wore a fedora and didn't look up. "Please come with us."

James held his ground.

"You will come with us."

James snapped, "Who are you?"

With his face to the pavement, the man implored, "Do as I say."

James looked toward the lead car, whose deep, tinted windows hid the identities of his pursuers. James looked around. He could make a run for it, but being shot in the streets didn't seem like a wise option. He took a calculated risk and acquiesced. "Very well." He was hustled into the rear car, bookended by the two men.

The driver ordered, "Lay down now."

James turned to the fedora man, and said, "So this is a kidnapping?"

The fedora man remained reticent.

The third man demanded with authority, "Give me your cell phone."

James complied and the man placed the phone in a metal box so it couldn't be tracked.

As James lay down, they darted off. A few minutes passed and they drove into a dark parking garage.

The driver curtly spit out, "Sit up."

James popped up and the two men whisked him out of one car and into another car driven by an attractive woman, with dark-chocolate eyes and olive skin, who cocked her head. She whispered, "Lay back down, please."

"Where are we going?"

The driver adjusted her mirror, tilting it down so they made eye contact.

The fedora man demanded, "Don't ask questions."

"I'll ask whatever I want. I came peacefully after all."

The driver squinted but the two captors remained taciturn. The car lurched off.

After forty minutes passed, they made it to the countryside.

"You may sit up now." The woman driver turned up a long, fenced drive and sped toward an ornate gate that secured the estate's exterior. It opened without request as they headed onto a beautiful estate.

Chapter 39

The driver stopped at the base of a series of steps leading to massive Doric columns that guarded a colossal mansion.

An armed guard opened the door for James and escorted him up the steps and into a sitting room three stories high. Tapestries hung from the ceiling; furniture worthy of a sheik decorated the room.

James noticed gold inlays were sculpted into the marble flooring. Each shuffling step echoed in the expansive chamber. An impressive sight, but James felt the room lacked warmth. It had the pretentious and grandiose appeal of the nouveau riche.

From behind James, a voice asked, "Drink, Your Highness?"

James turned to see Al Hassan dressed in a blue suit without a tie. His tan, woven sandals caught his eye. Sophisticated but casual.

"No, thank you."

Al Hassan lifted his own glass. "Please, don't let me drink alone." He smiled and gestured one more time.

"Very well."

"I hope you appreciate Strathbury."

James cued, "From the royal vineyard?"

"One and the same." He snapped his finger and a woman servant tapped the tile with her heels, carrying a tray with a second glass and a bottle of wine.

James took the glass as the woman poured wine for the prince. She bowed and left the room.

"One question?"

Al Hassan nodded.

"Am I free to leave?"

"Absolutely."

James turned to leave.

Al Hassan waved James's card. "But I understand you wanted a meeting."

"I do, but I'm only here because I didn't want to die."

"What makes you think I want you killed?"

"Why the elaborate train of cars to bring me here?"

"Let's just say you aren't the only one who fears for his life."

"Who do you fear?"

Al Hassan smiled. He held his finger to his lips to keep any further words from escaping the prince's lips. "Follow me."

They walked from hard flooring to a dark room. It had the warmth of a fireplace, ease of comfort furniture, and not a single window. In the center of the room a card table with two mismatched chairs.

Al Hassan approached a wall and tapped it. "Bug proof." He stepped close to James. "You wish to speak to me?"

James's gaze penetrated. "You brought me here."

"Fair enough, but it was you who came to my store, seeking me."

James raised his glass and said, "Very well, I want to ask why you have kept the inquest transcripts of my mother's and your son's death sealed. I want to know what you had to do with her death and with the death of the reporter."

Al Hassan tilted his head. "Reporter?"

"Hannister."

"You have me at a loss. I'm unfamiliar with that name."

James shook his head. "Hannister was about to expose you."

"For what?"

"For the crash that killed your son and my mother."

"Are you out of your mind? Ali was my only son."

"Then why seal the transcripts?"

Al Hassan and James studied each other in a game of cat and

mouse. Al Hassan circled the prince. "Do you think I have that ability? I have neither the desire to keep the transcripts under wraps nor the ability to seal them."

"But I was told you were responsible for keeping them sealed."

"Prince James, you have been misled. I can't even see the transcripts, and I'm not allowed to question my own employees about the events of my son's death. The truth, I'm afraid, remains elusive."

"Such as?" They sat at the table, looking at each other, not as opponents but as unwitting partners.

"Why weren't the experts for SUV allowed to examine the wrecked car? Why was the accident scene immediately street cleaned, thereby eliminating any physical evidence? And what about the other vehicles?"

James saw that Al Hassan had done his homework. "I assume you have made a commitment to the truth for your son's sake?"

Al Hassan stared and softly nodded.

"Well, I've made a similar commitment as well." James concurred.

"And you are aware of the dangers of such a pursuit?" probed Al Hassan.

"And what would those be, Mr. Hassan?"

Al Hassan smiled. "First, your earlier encounter should have told you something. Someone wants this swept under the rug. Second, the fire at your friend's shop. And third, have you read the tabloids today?"

James laughed. "Mr. Hassan, much of that is imaginative fodder by reporters creating fictional scoops."

"No, they are more than that. They are all warnings. Just as your encounter with thugs was a warning, so is the chipping away of your integrity. They call you a drunk and a drug addict, and worse." He reached into an ottoman and pulled a newspaper. "They call you this!" He held it up and the headline read, "Prince James: A Terrorist Target!"

James rebuked it, "How is that a warning?"

"Don't you see? What happened to you today will be in the paper tomorrow. Some random photograph will have been taken, and this caption will gain strength. If you become enough of a threat, then you will fall victim to a self-fulfilling prediction."

"A threat to whom?"

"Whoever killed your mother and my son, that's who." He continued. "And everyone, myself included, is expendable; even you have a brother who can replace you."

James bristled, "Who do you believe wanted to kill my mother?"

Mr. Al Hassan waved his hand. "I'm making no suggestions … yet. But remember, nothing happens in politics by accident."

James gazed at Al Hassan and defended his position. "Look, I don't know if you are part of the solution or part of the problem, but I do know that I want to get to the bottom of this. If I put my own life at risk, it's a risk I'm willing to take. Now, I need to see those transcripts if I'm going to solve this mystery."

Al Hassan nodded. "We agree. So we are united in a joint effort?" He silently lifted his drink.

With glass raised, James saluted. "We have found some common terrain."

Al Hassan in agreement slowly drained his glass.

Chapter 40

James's VW Rabbit rolled into the parking garage ahead of his security detail. He made his way to the penthouse. As the elevator opened, Woom stood with an impatient look.

She followed him as he continued in. "You have a polo match tomorrow. You and your brother will be playing."

"Good for Malcolm. How did he anchor a spot on the team?"

Woom perked up. "He's been sitting in for you at your position since you've been absent from practice."

"Is he any good?" James grinned.

"He doesn't have your tenacity."

James looked off. "No, I suspect he doesn't."

She reminded him. "The queen has requested your presence."

"I'm sure she has." He continued, working his way past the front room to the hallway.

Warden stood in the kitchen with his coat off, his shirtsleeves rolled to the elbow.

"What on earth are you doing, Warden?"

He turned and politely uttered in frustration, "I am fixing the garbage disposal."

"And why are you fixing it?"

"Because I broke it."

James entered the kitchen. "How?"

"Woom warned me to not dump an entire bowl of leftover beets in, but I did it anyway. I seem to have plugged the bloody thing up."

James changed the subject. "How come you aren't freaked out like everyone else?"

He winked. "James, to know you is to love you, and apparently, I'm the only one who knows you."

"When you get a chance, come see me in my room." James left Warden alone with his project and strolled away from Woom, who wouldn't leave his side.

As he put distance from her, Woom shouted, "Don't forget, tomorrow, early!"

An hour later Warden knocked and entered.

"Do you think there is any way I could avoid going to the polo match?"

Warden paused, his stare unblinking. "There is no way you can avoid it."

"Good Lord, I haven't been upon my steed in a month. I will embarrass myself."

"James, if I might be frank, practice is always important, but talent is as well. You are a very gifted player. You may not play up to your standards, but I most certainly doubt you will embarrass yourself." He came up alongside James. "Besides, you would be wise to pick your battles carefully. If you attend and behave as though nothing is amiss, it will keep the heat off of you."

James turned and studied his butler. "What makes you think something's amiss?"

Warden chided, "With you, something is always amiss."

"I'm serious, Warden. What do you know?"

"There's talk you've been digging deep. So be careful."

"Okay, I'll be there tomorrow. Do you think it would draw attention if I brought a woman with me?"

"Of course it would, but I suppose it would shift the suspicion off your mysterious outings and give peace of mind to the queen."

James wasn't so sure about that. This might be the dawn of a new era, but when she took one look at Alba, she might be a tad perturbed. "I can't wait to introduce her to the family."

Warden tilted his head with intrigue. "What does that mean?"

"She's a lovely woman. They will surely appreciate that."

"As much as I'd like to know more about her, I don't think you asked for my presence because of that. Is there something else on your mind?"

James swept his palms across his face, recounting the events of the day.

Warden further cautioned James. "You need to be careful."

"As do you, Warden. As do you. That is top secret, and I can't stress that more. Please do not tell anyone."

"James, you needn't worry about my loyalty, only about your safety."

"I understand." James changed the subject. "May I have a sandwich? I have work to do, and don't plan on leaving the room."

Warden nodded. "Would you like a spot of tea as well?"

"Send something with an edge. I've had a rough day."

"Very well."

James remained in his room for the rest of the evening planning tomorrow. He missed his mother whose blood coursed through his body. Help me out here, Mum. I need you.

Chapter 41

The next morning, James donned the polo outfit Warden had set aside for him. He packed clothes into a carryall and slung it over his shoulder. He exited his room and strolled past the kitchen. He caught sight of something sticking up out of the sink and backpedaled. A plunger handle pointed upward like a flagstick. I see he's a better butler than a plumber. He laughed at the mess Warden left for himself. He grabbed a muffin from the refrigerator and gobbled it down.

When he made it to the basement, a silver stretch Rolls Royce waited for him. He watched his reflection in the glass slowly disappear as his grandmother lowered the window.

"Care to join me?"

"Thanks, but that's not necessary, Grandmother."

The queen, not given to bouts of smiling, grimly offered the faintest Mona Lisa expression. "Indulge me, please."

James hesitated. "It would be my pleasure." He gestured to Harold, the royal chauffeur, and released his bags to the servant's care. James circled the car as Harold attended to the door.

"Here you are, Your Highness."

In the comfort of the coach, James sat opposite the queen. The two of them offered little conversation. The matriarch had a sour expression and lifted a panel beside her. She retrieved a cigarette and pushed the lighter downward on the console. "I love this invention," she muttered to herself.

James watched as she held the cherry red end of the lighter against the tip of her cigarette. His grandmother took a long drag and exhaled a gray cloud into the enclosed chamber.

James toggled the window and gave himself some breathing room. James offered, "You know, Granny, if you don't quit those, they are going to make you sick."

She took another long drag before setting it in an ashtray. She ignored his comment then stated, "James, our family has ruled for over five hundred years. Five hundred years of tradition." She grinned as though she found it amusing. "And you and I are the connective tissue. I followed my father to the throne, and so shall you."

James asked, "Do you worry that we're an anachronism?"

She bellowed, "Dear James. We are the elite. As for those republics who claim to have no royalty, they are craven hypocrites. They just conceal their inequities with the veneer of democracy."

"That may be true, but are we any better?"

"You know, James, I've dedicated my life to defending the realm from any threat." She held him in her gaze. "Any threat. You understand that, don't you, James?"

James nodded. "Yes." He offered, "If we are ever threatened, I will stand beside you."

She reached out and patted James's hand. "Let us take care of it. I promise we are doing all we can. With Louis and Gardenia's wedding coming up, we need things to run smoothly."

The car slowed and James could see the entrance to the polo grounds. They slipped back into their own worlds. When Harold opened the door, the queen politely ushered her grandson out. As he stood there, she offered, "James, there are dark forces over which we have no control."

James took his gear and clothing and made his way past a parking lot of the most expensive cars on the market. Grandmother was right. He was set to play a game only enjoyed by the elite. His thoughts weighed heavily, but hearing the soft voice of Alba behind him pulled him out of his concern. He turned to see her radiant smile. As much

as he promised he would resist his urges, he had no control as he gravitated to her and kissed her on the cheek, squeezing her lithe frame
against his. "Thank you for coming."

"I wouldn't miss this, James."

He whispered, "I have the inquest transcripts' case number. I'm
going after them today."

"Fantastic." Then she whispered, "Just make sure to only use the
terminal at the counter."

"You'll need this to get in," he said as he casually handed her
a small envelope. "It's an ID badge to get in to any government
facility."

Behind him, a Range Rover screeched to a halt. James turned to
see Malcolm scramble out, looking older than his nineteen years. He
had an irrepressible grin on his face as he approached James and Alba.
His eyes widened as he assessed Alba from toe to head. He winked at
James and gave Alba a peck on the cheek. "Please tell me you aren't
here with my dear brother."

"Guilty as charged."

"You are smashing." He turned to his brother. "And she would be?"

"This is Alba."

Malcolm took her hand and said, "Malcolm Henry George
Edward Arthur Spencer Merlin. I come from a very long line of very
dead people. But rest assured, I am at your service."

But Malcolm continued to linger beside them, unmoved by the
subtle gestures from his brother to scram.

James offered up, "I see my brother has forgotten his antipsychotic
medication today."

Malcolm sneered and put his arm around Alba's shoulder. "Come
root for me instead of Mr. Morbid."

"You strike me as a young man with plenty of women."

"Ouch. Do you know how hard it is to meet a woman on a totally
honest plane?"

"I'm sure it's not that tough. Besides, I have somewhere else to be."
She turned to James and smiled. "Well, I'm off."

James wanted to wrap his arms around her in a gesture of good-bye but just nodded. "Take care, Alba."

Malcolm shouted, "Stay healthy!" He turned to his brother and whispered, "You stay healthy too. Being king would be my worst nightmare. Plus I would be King Malcolm X."

James grinned and patted his brother on the shoulder. "Don't worry Malc. I'm in good health."

Malcolm drew a bead on his brother. "I'm picking up rumors all over town about you and ..."

"Alba?"

"You and mother."

"Really?"

"Is there something you want to tell me?" Malcolm stood in James's path to the polo grounds.

Then from a distance, a rider shouted, "Get up here! We need a little time with our best player!"

Malcolm jested, "I'll be right there!"

Two other riders snickered. "Not you. Make sure James is ready."

Malcolm frowned. "Did you hear that? I've been practicing and I still can't get the respect you do." Then he got serious. "Is there something I should know?"

"Malc, do you want to know the truth or do you want to be happy?"

Malcolm held his hands out as though they were a weighing scale. "Can't I be both?"

James slapped his brother on the shoulder. They hurried on without finishing that discussion.

Chapter 42

James found himself distracted, and his polo playing showed it. His brother outshone him that day, and the ribbing from his teammates continued until Warden picked him up to leave. The security detail accompanied Warden.

"James, if you need any lessons, let me know." Malcolm winked and the two embraced quickly before James jumped in with Warden.

"How did the match go?"

James shrugged. "As expected." He looked over at Warden. "So how did your meeting go?"

Warden kept a steady hand on the wheel. "Let's just say I've been reminded that my job involves keeping you out of trouble. Trouble being a rather broadly interpreted word."

James tilted his head and looked in the side-view mirror at the detail behind him. "Did Grandmother say anything to Vern and Rex?"

Warden didn't flinch. "Vex and Rern? Plenty."

"Well, I'm going to need your help this afternoon."

Warden's face lost expression. "Can't we wait a day or two?"

"We cannot."

"And what is my role?"

"I need you to make Vern and Rex believe I'm in this car tonight."

"And why is that?"

"Let's just say, I have a little covert operation planned."

They made it home and James contacted Colin. "Col, I need some assistance today."

Colin's voice had a tired edge. His bookstore weighed heavy on his heart.

James assured him. "Don't worry, friend. we'll have your bookstore up and running in no time."

"James, you don't have to do that. I'm insured."

"Ah yes, but let's upgrade it a tad."

"It's not necessary."

"Nothing in life is necessary except food, air, and water. And last time I checked, you have plenty of those."

"We'll discuss it. What do you need me for?"

James needed Colin to come to a location dressed exactly as ordered. James would explain later. "And don't be late. I need you there early, and I need you to park somewhere discreet."

Shortly before 4:00 p.m., James and Warden prepared to head out for an appointment. James grabbed his overcoat and tossed a scarf around his neck. He concealed his face with a brimmed hat. The detail followed close behind as they drove downtown to the inspector general's office.

Chapter 43

Lime-green walls and fluorescent lighting gave the inspector general's office a dingy, bureaucratic feel. People stood patiently waiting in two lines as attendants sat behind windows while addressing requests.

James knew not to make his identity obvious or he might receive preferential treatment with a computer terminal other than the one Alba instructed him to use. He scanned the room. Colin, you'd better be here.

No sooner had the thought crossed his mind, Colin tapped him on the shoulder. "Looking for me?"

"Good man." They exchanged hats, Colin's ball cap for James's fedora. They exchanged coats, and James circled the scarf around Colin's neck. "Be me!" James turned to Warden, who watched the exchange with amusement. "Better get going before Vern and Rex decide to come up."

Colin shuffled alongside Warden as they exited.

James could only hope he'd fooled his detail.

As the numbers thinned, James made it to the counter and a young woman wearing a white blouse and nametag asked, "Aren't you …"

"Yes, I am, but I'd like to keep it a secret." James drew the bill of the cap down.

"I see. How may I help you?"

James grabbed a request form and wrote out a number. "I'd like to get a copy of case number 322-1963-JK."

The woman pivoted to the screen and typed with efficient speed. Her eyes scanned the screen as her expression sunk.

"Is there a problem?"

"System's been slow all day." She pounded a key and started re-typing. "Let's try it again." She waited another minute. "Sorry, it's also been a bit glitchy as well." She feigned a smile and explained, "It must be a huge file because it is taking its time cycling up." She tapped her fingers against the counter, a syncopation of press-on nails against Formica. "Bravo! Here it is."

Then she frowned.

"Yes?"

"It says 322-1963-JK is a restricted file by order of the inspector general."

"I am the prince, you know."

She sighed. "I know, but not even Jesus could get this file if the inspector general has it restricted." She handed him a form. "If you fill this out, a notification will be sent to you within ninety days."

James chuckled at the absurdity. "No, that would not be timely."

She whispered, "I don't set policy or I would let you have it; however, I don't have that authority. I have to have my supervisor unlock this file."

"I see."

She paused, looked about, and continued. "By the way, I admired Princess Christina very much. She was the best thing about the royal family." She put her hand to her lips. "Excuse me, present company excluded."

"Thank you for the kind words about my mother." James turned and noticed the room had emptied. He was the last citizen requesting official records. Besides the young woman starting to close down, only a janitor remained.

Cloaked in blue coveralls and dark blue ball cap, the female janitor kept her face to the ground and busily mopped.

James smiled. He recognized her gait.

He left the room and made his way to the janitor's utility room. He closed the door behind him and waited for the building to empty.

By five thirty, every government employee filtered out to either the waiting arms of a significant other or the frosty mug of a brew.

James peeked out the door to a quiet, lonely hallway. He made his way back to the inspector general's office. As he suspected, Alba had left the door unlocked.

Inside, she worked over a computer, her face a ghostly electric blue.

James whispered as she looked up at him, "The clerk said it requires a supervisor's password."

"Already cracked it."

"That quickly?"

"Just have to know where to look. I've already been to the supervisor's desk. He's not the sharpest tool in the shed. He kept it on his desktop in a folder called ..." She grinned. "Passwords."

James made his way to the radiant light coming from the screen. "Do you have the file?"

"Working on it." Just like the young clerk, Alba lamented that the computer was slow. "Damn thing is walking in mud."

James heard a door open from down the hall. "That's the night watchman doing his rounds."

"Got it!" She moused the file and clicked to copy. "Come on, file."

James watched as the file exchanged percentages, fifteen percent complete.

Another door slammed and keys jingled.

Twenty-five percent complete.

Another door opened and closed.

He whispered, "You better hurry."

As the night watchman approached, the percentage neared one hundred. As the computer whirled and dinged, she pulled the flash drive and with no time left yanked the plug so the computer would darken the room.

Then the doorknob turned.

James grabbed Alba and pulled her on top and started kissing her.

"Who's in here?" The night watchman's flashlight caught the

two bandits in an amorous embrace. He flipped the room light on and stared at James. "What are you doing … Is that you, Prince James?"

James feigned embarrassment. "Sorry." He stood and rescued his fallen cap. "So very embarrassed."

As Alba tucked the drive into her pocket as though nothing more than an indiscretion had taken place.

James caught the guard's attention. "May I have a word with you?"

Alba grabbed her mop and bucket, rolled it past the guard and out the door.

James came up alongside the guard with a hundred euro note. "I'd be very embarrassed if this leaked to the public, you know, reputation and all."

The guard nodded with a sense of awe. "Understood, sir." He took the bill with a subtle glance and quietly secreted it away. The guard offered, "But this is a government building and perhaps not the best place to exercise one's libido."

"I couldn't agree more." He shook the guard's hand. "Won't happen again. Huge mistake."

The guard straightened up. "Well, see that it doesn't."

James smiled, bowed his head, and trotted to the door. As he made it to the elevator, Alba had her coverall off and waited with the door open.

"Huge mistake?"

James pushed the ground floor button. "I had to say something."

Alba shook her head and grinned.

James opined, "Pretty glamorous, huh?" He felt proud. "Sometimes I have to think like a criminal."

Alba cautioned him. "I have a criminal mind, but I try not to use it."

James scoffed, "At least not too much."

Alba sighed. "Why are royals so crazy?"

As the elevator hit the ground floor and the door opened, James laughed. "We're not crazy. We're fun!"

Chapter 43

When they made it to Alba's apartment, James checked his text messages. Warden wanted to know when he could officially quit driving Colin around. James messaged back, "Drop by Alba's. We can make an identity swap."

Alba opened the flash drive and began printing all the pages of the transcript. "I'll separate all the witness testimonies."

James studied the growing pile. "Looks like that's going to take a while."

"Do you have a better plan?"

"Let's separate them into before and after the crash."

"We can separate them as many ways as you like."

"Well, by person and by sequence. That way, we can construct a timeline."

Alba smiled and went about creating a document that told a tale much deeper than the public realized.

Before long, a knock at the door brought in Colin and Warden, with the detail downstairs in a waiting car.

James ordered Warden, "We need all hands on deck. I'm looking for anything out of the ordinary." He dropped a pile of post-accident testimony in front of Warden.

Warden asked, "Unusual as in more unusual than an accident?"

"Something like that."

Colin chimed in, "Where's my stack?"

"Here." Alba plopped another pile down onto the couch. "Make yourself comfortable."

James handed them red pencils. "Anything that doesn't fit, mark it." James turned and spoke to everyone. "The timeline is crucial. Mother and Ali Hassan arrived at the hotel around 8:00 p.m."

Alba suggested, "Let me brew some coffee."

Warden intervened. "Do you have tea?"

"Earl Grey or Oolong?"

Warden stood. "Lead me to the kitchen. I will prepare it all."

Alba's eyes lit up. "If this is what help is like, I'll take two of you, Warden."

"Thank you, madam."

She scowled. "But if you call me madam again, we will have a short friendship."

"Yes, ma ... Yes, Ms. Alba."

She sighed. "Please, just Alba."

Warden turned and bowed. "Very well, Just Alba." Warden winked.

Alba snickered and turned to James. "Oh, your butler has a sense of humor."

James kept studying a file. "That he does. When he likes you."

James started a timeline and called out what he knew as he drew it up on a tablet. "After they arrived at 8:00 p.m., they had dinner at 9:00. Everyone have that?"

Alba nodded, but Colin shook his head. "9:30."

James revisited his doc. "Alba, what do you have?"

"Closer to 9:30."

James crossed out a timeline entry and wrote, "9:30." "Next, they left the hotel at 12:15 a.m."

Colin again took exception. "Actually they left at exactly 12:17."

James stiffened and stared at his friend. "How can you be so certain?"

Colin held up a photo and a magnifying glass. "Look at the window."

James grabbed the photo and eyed it with a magnifying glass.

Reflected in the window was the backward image of a streaming digital clock on the Horford Hotel that was across the street. "Interesting." He continued. "That means they only had six minutes before the crash." He held up the official report from several witnesses who heard the accident at 12:23. "So that means if our media sources are correct and the SUV left the paparazzi in the dust, they didn't slow down even when they were away from the paparazzi. Which would mean Mother's bodyguard, Clare Thornton-Smith, was correct. They still had a hard tail on them."

Warden walked in with a tray of coffee, tea, sugar, and cream. "She said they were being pursued by someone besides the paparazzi?"

"Yes, she did, Warden." James took a heavy breath. "What happened on that bridge?"

Colin interrupted. "Do any of the other victims' autopsy reports have carbon monoxide poisoning?"

James thumbed through his mother's report, while Alba searched Ali Hassan's. "No carbon monoxide here. How about Ali, Alba?"

She shook her head. "Why do you ask, Colin?"

Colin stated, "Because the driver Cromwell Clay-Bauer's labs looks like he smoked the exhaust pipe. His blood had twenty-four percent carbon monoxide. Could the crashed car have created a pocket of carbon monoxide?"

"With twenty-four percent CO blood level, he would have been semiconscious, let alone able to walk or drive. Everyone else in the car had none." James twisted with uneasiness. "No, even had the car remained running, which it most certainly did not, that's too open an area to intoxicate someone that quickly."

Warden put down the tray, distributed the drinks, and picked up a file. He opened it and flipped over several pages. "Well, Mr. Clay-Bauer was not the only person that night with high monoxide poisoning and a blood alcohol level over 0.2."

James stepped toward Warden and looked into the folder. "Someone else in the car suffered the same high levels?"

Warden pointed to an entry. "No, but someone else came into the emergency department and died that night. One George Debord."

James repeated the name "George Debord." He thought out loud, "Why does that name sound familiar?" He stared into space, trying to recall. He clapped his hands together in victory. "I know that name! The psychic, Colleen Cutter, said a Debord was somehow involved."

Warden scoffed and Colin backed him up. "A psychic, James?"

"Say what you will, but whatever the source, she pointed it out and for good reason."

Colin cautioned, "Careful, James. Perhaps she's given you a red herring."

"She said, 'CO Debord.' CO equals carbon monoxide. The psychic called it and came up aces."

"Maybe, one way or another, something is being covered up." Colin turned the page and asked Warden, "Do we know the circumstances of Debord's death?"

Warden read aloud. "Debord came in with self-asphyxiation from carbon monoxide, as well as a high alcohol level and massive amount of antidepressant drugs. Suicide."

James uttered, "Interesting. That's what the autopsy report on Clay-Bauer says." He asked, "Is there a toxicology report with levels listed?"

Warden said, "Yes. Here."

James gathered them and read them.

Alba asked, "Is it possible they mixed the test results?"

James smiled. "Mixed? Don't you mean substituted?" He handed her the reports. "Both men's results were identical. They replaced Clay-Bauer's toxicology results with Debord's. That way, Clay-Bauer could be accused of driving impaired."

"Was a DNA test done on the sample?" Colin inquired.

"No, there was a request by Clay-Bauer's family but by then the sample had been destroyed," Warden added.

The four of them looked at each other in silence. No one could deny that there appeared to be a conspiracy. Now they needed to know who the intended target was.

Colin interrupted. "I don't mean to add fuel to this query, but look at this." He placed his file on the table and highlighted a passage. "The detective in charge of the investigation stated that night that Clay-Bauer had 5,000 euros in cash on his person. And had made a recent bank deposit of 8,000 euros." Colin looked up. "What kind of salary did Clay-Bauer earn?"

James answered, "About 25,000 a year."

Colin asked, "So where did he get that kind of money?"

Alba inquired, "Who gave him that kind of money?"

James had an uneasy feeling. "They were going to Ali's apartment, but instead Clay-Bauer took a less direct route and drove them onto the Old Boston Bridge. He went to the grave not knowing who pulled his strings."

Alba joined Warden and James, standing behind Colin, peering down at the folder. "What do you mean?"

James concluded, "I think Bauer was a pawn."

She continued. "I'd say Clay was molded."

James and Colin smiled, and even Warden raised an eyebrow.

Chapter 44

Colin took his leave. He needed to find his way home to Eliza. Then Warden asked if he could rest his eyes on the couch.

As James and Alba continued their research, James noticed how peaceful Warden looked. He'd never taken the time to understand that all those who worked in the service of the royal family had another side to them. Warden lay supine with a throw pillow under his head. James removed a blanket from the backrest and placed it over his sleeping body.

"He's sure a nice man." Alba waited as James gently tucked the edges around his shoulders.

"Yeah, he's always been there for me, through a lot of ups and downs."

When they were alone, James had a chance to say something. "Thanks for everything." He found himself nervous. He wanted to show his gratitude but didn't want to push his feelings.

"Well, Alba, what have you been working on?"

She had brought up footage from the surveillance cameras located outside the Grand Hotel. "As you can see, we have an entire view of what happened in front of the hotel." She pointed to a couple of vehicles: a white sedan and a dark sedan. "From the security cameras, it appears certain they were being stalked."

"Didn't the witnesses identify a motorcycle as well?"

"It comes into the picture in a second." They watched as the crowded street of onlookers watched the princess and Ali depart in their SUV, followed by a white sedan and a dark sedan. "Right there!" She pointed as a motorcycle with two people darted out ahead of the dark luxury car. "There is the motorcycle."

"That's not paparazzi."

"How can you be so certain?"

"Look at the driver. He's driving a café-style racer and he clearly knows how to ride it. Hell, a reporter would kill himself on that. Plus the passenger is leaning with the driver. Those are pros." James sighed. "I'd like to know who they are."

Alba reversed the video and zoomed in on the motorcycle's license plate. "I think I can clean that up enough to read it. But if they are pros, I suspect those will be stolen plates."

"Maybe, but it's a place to start."

Alba nodded. "You got it." She handed him a photocopy of the white sedan. "Here is the plate for the white car."

"Alba, what about all the traffic cameras along the route that night?"

"Great point. There were ten cameras along the road leading to the bridge and seventeen cameras on the bridge."

"Fantastic."

"Do you want to see the videos?"

"Let's go."

"All right. Here's camera 1." Alba hit her keyboard.

On her computer, the screen appeared completely black.

"Here's camera 2." Alba struck her keyboard again.

Her computer screen remained black.

"Camera 3 ..."

Just as she raised her finger, James interrupted her. "Let me guess. So all the cameras were inoperative that night?"

"Exactly. On the night your mother died, between 12:20 and 12:45 a.m., all twenty-seven cameras were off. According to the traffic department, 'For maintenance.'"

James pondered this revelation. Who is hiding what? And how high does this go?

He placed a gentle hand on her shoulder as he leaned over her back and peered into the screen. "You're the best."

She reached up and squeezed one of his fingers. "Thanks." She scrolled to the end of the video.

"We've been lucky thanks to you, Alba."

"That's a first. I've never been lucky. My father worried my luck would never change. He feared my end would come as a result of my bad luck." She looked at James with reluctance, as though she feared something between them. "I think this is the beginning of my luck changing." She twisted in her chair and glanced into his eyes.

James avoided those dalliance questions. He offered, "I hope so."

"You know, you're completely different than I thought."

James straightened up and looked down at her. "Is that a good or bad thing?"

Her eyes sparkled and her smile widened. "You do your mother proud."

He lamented, "She saw what happened to my father. He is not strong. He's controlled. In the royal house, it's easy to become insulated ... detached. Mum wasn't going to let that happen to Malc and me. She raised us to live life, to seize it and see it fully. The good and the bad. She wanted us to make a difference. Put a dent in the status quo. I've spent the last four years wallowing in my selfishness, ignoring my mother's voice."

As James stared down at Alba, his heart grew heavy. "My mum was shocked by the opposition she faced. For every person who argued against her suggestions, none was as damning as those from my own family."

Alba stood and reached up to James's face, placing a hand on his cheek. "It nice to hear you talking about her. You bring her alive with your memories."

"Alba, in your book you never explicitly stated why this tragedy happened."

"I believe they didn't want her to be the power behind the throne when you became king."

"But she was a loving, compassionate person. It makes no sense."

"Because she was for peace."

James patted her hand then subtly dabbed his eye with his finger. "I didn't realize how much of her I carried inside. I thought I'd extinguished it, but she's a restless soul and she will never leave me."

The moment was cut short. As a call came in, Alba's phone danced on vibrate, sliding across the desk.

James reached down and picked up the phone. He stared at the screen. The number was unmistakable. "My father is calling your phone?" His heart raced to a betrayed conclusion. He looked at her and asked, "Why is my father calling you?"

Alba shrunk back. "Don't answer it."

James tripped the on button.

"Please." Alba pleaded.

James put the phone to his ear. "Father." He listened before releasing the phone to Alba. "It's for you."

She tried to end the call, answering in short bursting responses.

James had pulled Warden awake and pushed him out the door. He barely gave her thirty seconds time before he'd cleared himself of her presence.

As James gathered his senses in the hall, Warden puzzled, "What's going on?"

James barged in the elevator and hit, "Ground."

Warden put his arm on James's shoulder. "What happened, James?"

"I don't know who to trust anymore."

They come to the ground floor, where Vern waited in the lobby. He whispered into his mouthpiece and led the way out to the street.

James's phone rang and he pulled it out of his pocket. Alba's caller ID appeared. "Her." He showed Warden the screen.

"I don't understand, James."

The two men put on their coats, buttoning up against the chill of an offshore breeze. James let the phone ring through, but she called again.

As they entered Warden's car, James finally shut the phone down.

Warden kept his eyes trained on the road before the headlamps.

James shook his head in disgust. How could she? Does my family have me under control?

"I've known you all your life, James, and one thing I know, you are most bothered when you are at your quietest."

"Then I guess I shall go mute."

Warden trained his gaze back to the road.

"So is this a matter of the heart?"

"It isn't that. It's that I trusted her. I always seem to trust the wrong people."

He liked Alba. There was an energy to her that made him feel alive. But this had more to do with the possibility that someone planted her in his path, to keep him controlled. He explained the phone call from his father.

"You are basing an awful lot on a phone call. The woman I've met certainly isn't trying to stop you from discovering the truth about your mother." Warden offered, "Always talk things out before you storm off, because if you don't, someone will be shortchanged. Remember what your mother used to say ..."

James took over. "'When you find someone you truly love, who makes you happy, hold on tight.'" James stared out into the city night. "It's times like this that I miss, Mum."

"Your mother was a wonderful woman. I truly wish you could have a conversation with her."

James's head snapped around. A revelation came to him. "You're right! And I think I can."

"Excuse me?"

James slid next to Warden and messed his hair. "You always have the subtle answer."

"I think even I missed that one." Warden appeared confused.

"If my mother kept a diary, she may be able to answer a lot of my questions."

Warden smiled. "And if she did keep one, James. It would be in the Albion Depository Warehouse."

James grinned. "Perfect."

Chapter 45

Early came early. James woke with the rising sun, his thoughts mixed between his mother's diaries and a feeling for someone who played him for a fool. He dismissed them.

He let his staff sleep; however, the watchful eyes of Vern and Rex waited below. Vern had watch. A sleeping Rex, head tilted back with his mouth pushing out a snore that reverberated throughout the basement garage.

James nodded and raised a cup of coffee. "Cheers!"

Vern answered, "Awfully early to be about." As he wiped his face and pushed off from the car. The two men met halfway to James's car. "Everything okay?"

James hesitated but smiled. "Yeah, yeah, I'm fine. Thanks for asking. How are you boys doing out here?"

"Other than never knowing if we've lost you, and are going to be reamed by the queen, not bad."

"You needn't worry. I'm headed to the Albion Depository."

"Well, I'd better wake Grumpy and tell him you're on the move."

They grinned and started up their separate cars.

James started early knowing the task of finding something of his mother's might be a protracted process.

The Albion Depository was a series of connected warehouses,

each two stories high with fifteen-foot shelving stacked with the history of the crown. For the most part, the process of digitizing had not gone far and the records were still stored on large, handwritten ledgers.

James flipped through the order of names, dates, and locations. An entry noted his mother's belongings stored in the last building. He walked through a series of automatic glass doors. He carefully passed through the last door, which opened electrically. By every door there were water coolers topped with five-gallon glass bottles.

James looked up at the rows of shelves filled with of numbered boxes bearing his mother's three scallops coat of arms.

When he came to the last row, there leaning against a ladder, a nervous Alba waited. James narrowed his gaze. "Why are you here?"

Alba blinked as though she'd been there all night. "Warden said you would be coming, so I made my way here to talk with you."

"I see you used the badge I gave you, or has my father allowed you to come and go?"

She bowed her head and placed her dark sunglasses over her weariness. "I suppose I deserve that." Her voice echoed off the concrete flooring. "But you are wrong."

"About?" He passed her and climbed the ladder. He read off a number and matched it to a box on the top row.

She stood beneath him and called up, "Please come down and let me explain."

He was not the fool she took him for, but the first time since his mother's death, he felt deeply crushed.

James pulled a box out and cut through the tape. As he looked at the contents, he mumbled, "Everything is fine. There's nothing to explain."

"It's not fine. Please come down."

As he turned from the box, he lost his grip. The box tumbled downward. In an instinctual need to protect her, James yelled, "Look out!"

But she couldn't move quickly enough to evade the twenty-pound box that bounced off her shoulder.

"Alba. I'm so sorry." He placed his feet on the railings of the ladder and slid down with the grace of a fireman descending a pole. As he came to the ground, he leaned down to a fallen Alba. "Are you okay?" He forgot his sense of betrayal and put his arm around her.

She fell into his chest and sobbed. "James, I'm so sorry. I promise I am in this with you, and only with you."

"Shh, it's okay."

She pulled away and looked into his face. "It's not okay, I need you to believe me."

James lifted some fallen baby shoes and a stuffed rabbit. He started repacking the box. "You know, everyone in my life eventually betrays me. I hoped you would be different."

"I would never betray you."

"And yet my father calls you."

Alba sat on bottom rung of the ladder and removed her sunglasses. "When I first researched my book, I contacted many people. Your father was one of them. He wouldn't let me quote him but we spoke about his loss and how hard it was on you. He kept my number. When he saw us together, he asked me to keep him informed. But I promise you I never considered telling him anything."

"Why didn't you tell me that?"

Alba looked at James as though she saw a ghost. "Because I'm worried you and I may have different ideas of who can help, or who was involved."

Before James could respond, a voice startled them. "What are you doing here, James?"

James turned and Prince Richard came into view. Alba and James froze.

"Well?"

"Just going through a few of Mother's papers."

Prince Richard raised his eyebrows. "I see." He followed the trail of spilled goods. "I hope you find what you are looking for."

"So do I." James stood up. "Grandfather, this is Alba Song."

Ignoring the remark as insignificant, his grandfather turned and walked away. With his back to them, his voice boomed through the hollow enclosure. "Make sure you put things in order so that nothing is misplaced." He turned and stared at James. "And remember to look forward. That's the only thing that's important." Richard hit the doorplate, and when the door electrically opened, he stalked out.

James was surrounded by the only passage to his mother, and it only existed behind him, not forward.

Alba and James faced off; she stood and placed her glasses back on. "Well, take care, James." She rubbed her upper arm and turned away, walking past him and toward the main aisle.

James watched as she made her way around the corner. He shouted, "Wait!" He dropped the box. He caught up to her and found her quietly walking up to the door.

"What do you want, James?"

He smiled. "I was thinking …" He bowed his head and put his hands in his pockets.

"Yes?"

"How about a film tonight?"

She slid her glasses down and locked gazes with him.

"Only if I can buy the popcorn."

He grinned. "Of course."

Chapter 46

The brightly-lit theater marquee read,

"Obsession"
The Final Film Produced by Ali Hassan

James turned to Vern, who nodded and remained outside the theater. James had come to an agreement with his detail. He promised he would quit playing cat and mouse if they would not accompany him on his dates.

James and Alba skirted past the crowd and were let in as a perk to his nobility.

"Nice job of ditching the bodyguards." Alba pressed into James and held his arm tight.

"I didn't ditch them. Trust me. They will be waiting like sentries when we leave."

As they entered a nearly empty theater, James pulled a flask out of his coat and took four deep swallows.

Slowly the seats filled and they found themselves surrounded by a larger crowd than James expected.

Alba admitted, "Nice crowd."

"Yeah, I'm rather surprised."

They settled in as the lights went dark. Midway through the

coming attractions, James hollered in an inebriated voice, "Start the film! I'm running out of drink."

A small smattering of giggles rose, but as James continued, the tittering turned to muffled grumblings followed by the occasional "Shh."

A gentleman in front of him eventually turned and said, "Hey, some of us came to do a job."

Alba responded, "A job?"

"Yeah, this is the critics review night."

James whispered, "So that's why the heavy attendance." He rubbed Alba's hand and whispered, "Let's find out how well I can act."

A quick transformation. Now James spoke in a drunken slur. "I'm starting to sober up. Can't watch a film sober. Uncivilized."

"Shh. Shh. Shh. Shh."

Then the gentleman in front of him found it his duty to say something again, "Look, mister, I really would like to watch this movie in peace. Is that too much to ask?"

James slurred his words, "Do you know who I am?"

The man stood, leaned over the back of his seat, and narrowed the distance between them. "You are the drunken prince. Just shut up or leave."

A couple of patrons cheered, "Here! Here!" With a bow, the man took his seat again.

Just as the film began, James gave an exaggerated "Fine," and rose. He stumbled toward the aisle, tripping over a number of legs. "Pardon me ... Excuse me. Pardon me. Just recycling some nitrogen ..." When he made it to the aisle, he shouted, "Drinks for everyone!" He pointed at Alba and staggered his way to the exit.

When he cleared the room, he looked around and found the staircase to the theater offices. He knocked and the door swung open. A guard cleared a path, and inside was Al Hassan.

"I hope you weren't followed, Prince James."

"I don't think so." James thought the cloak and dagger was a bit much, but he wanted to reassure Mr. Hassan. "Besides, it looks like you are well protected."

"This is kid's help compared to the long arm of who could strike me."

"And who might that be?"

Al Hassan peered at James, his expression concealing something.

"Very well. Here is your copy of the transcripts." James stepped up to Al Hassan and handed him a flash drive.

Al Hassan smiled with relief, as though a weight of many years had fallen off his shoulders. "Well done. Very well done." He held it like a prize. "So have you read it?"

"Of course."

"And what did you think?"

James felt his own heavy thoughts weighing on him. "I know what happened that night on the bridge. The suppressed testimony proves there was a complete cover-up. Now I want to know by whom and why?"

Al Hassan laughed in absurdity. "Who and why? You want to know?"

James held his arms out. "If you know, then tell me."

Al Hassan motioned James to sit down. Then he gazed at James as though trying to understand him. "You really have no idea who did this, do you?"

"It's why I'm here."

"Were you aware your mother and my son were having an affair?"

James shook his head. "That's absurd. My mother and father would never have cheated on each other."

"Your father did know. Because he was having an affair with Gardenia Morgan-Bowen. Your mother was going to leave him."

James dismissed it. "That's not possible."

"And your mother was pregnant."

James looked up aghast. "Bullshit."

Al Hassan's face never flinched. "That's why Christina was illegally embalmed before an autopsy was performed. To conceal her pregnancy."

James sighed. "And if she was, are you insinuating that someone in my family did this? Over a pregnancy?"

"They didn't want you to have a nigger sibling." Al Hassan clasped his hands together and motioned his guard to leave the room. When they were alone, he opened up. "Christina and my son were deeply involved." He held his hand up in objection. "But that is not why your mother wanted out of the marriage. My son was not the cause of the marital unhappiness in your family."

"Even if my parents were unhappy, we are talking about murder, not from some terrorist group but from my family, her family."

"Her married family."

"So the blood family of her sons." James found himself defensive. "Just tell me who you think ordered the hit."

Al Hassan swiveled to window peering over the city below. "I suspect it was ordered by the most vicious and racist member of your family … Prince Richard."

Chapter 47

James tried to absorb Al Hassan's information. If his father knew of his mother's pregnancy, would he have also known that Richard ordered her death? Could his father and grandmother be in danger as well?

He made it back to Alba and pretended to sleep.

The film end credits rolled. Like all good critics, no one applauded except James. Loudly. The man in front of him turned and sarcastically quipped, "Your Highness, your family would be quite proud of you."

James retorted, "Don't worry. The white wine came up with the fish."

The gentleman shook his head and dismissed himself.

Alba nudged James. "Your performance was better than any on the screen."

They made their way to the street. Vern and Rex waited in their car next to James's VW Rabbit. He came up to the passenger window and Vern asked, "Any good?"

"Not really. Hey, can you guys not follow me tonight. I'd like a little time alone. I promise to come home as soon as I drop off Alba."

Vern turned to Rex who grumbled but acquiesced. "Very well, but if you aren't back in an hour, we will raid her apartment." Vern smiled.

James tapped the roof and said, "Good night, guys."

James and Alba waited for his detail to leave. "You want to walk?"

Alba smirked. "From here?"

James said, "It's not that far. Besides, it's a beautiful night."

Alba embraced his arm. "Lead the way, charmer. Besides, something tells me there's something on your mind."

"There is."

"About?"

"Al Hassan has accused my grandfather."

Alba didn't say a word.

James noticed her lack of engagement. "Do you agree?"

She widened her eyes and nodded.

As they walked, James couldn't help but notice the blue cast over them from moonlight, a peaceful, easy, calming effect.

"You know," Alba suggested, "lately I always feel as though I'm being followed."

James looked skyward at the full moon. "You know somewhere there's a Sea of Tranquility."

"But it's right next to the Sea of Crisis."

"Uh huh." James pointed and asked, "See that yellow star right below the moon?"

Alba squinted and shrugged.

"That's Saturn. My family puts a lot of importance in it."

"Saturn is also called Kronos, the father of time," Alba retorted. "Saturnalia is the Roman festival leading to the winter solstice, the coming of the light. Many believe its practice of giving gifts led to your Christmas."

James looked at her. "I'm impressed."

They held hands, swinging them as they enjoyed each other's company. When they made it to her apartment building, James thought the time went too quickly.

"I should get back. I don't want Vern and Rex barging in on us." He turned and faced her as they stood at the front entrance to her building. They gazed at each other and Alba closed her eyes. Had James not committed himself to her integrity, he would have carried her upstairs and spent the night. He broke away and said, "Well, I better go before something wonderful happens."

Alba let out a huge breath. "Yeah, no complications."

He watched as she slid her card through the lock and opened the door. She turned and pressed her hands against the door as James turned to leave.

He bowed his head and swiped the stress from his face. Could his grandfather have killed his mother?

He just made it to the corner when two drunken men bumped into him, knocking him against the stone side of a building.

"Pardon me, guys."

A burly man with a hunting jacket said, "Hey, do you know who you are?"

James passed it off. "I get that all the time. He's a bit taller."

The second man, taller, leaner, stepped forward. "No, no, you're him. I know it."

The first man huffed. "You've a good life, money, sheilas, no cares."

"Trust me, you're mistaken."

The taller one shook his head. "You calling my mate a liar?"

James realized they weren't as drunk as they appeared. They'd played the drunken role just as he had.

The two men separated slightly, boxing him against the wall. The first man put his hand against the wall and leaned in so James was only inches away. His cheap cologne danced between them. "Leave the dead buried if you don't want to join them."

The second man grabbed James shirt and slugged him in the stomach. "Word to the wise, understood?"

James hunched over and held his stomach. He looked up and grunted, "Fuck you."

"Oh, fuck me, huh?" The man grabbed James hair and pulled him standing. He cocked his fist back to deliver a blow when someone flashed from the shadows. The figure smashed the second man in the mouth and kicked him in the crotch, laying him to the ground.

James caught his wind to see Kerry Bolles barging into the scrum.

Bolles turned to the first man and whispered in mock disapproval. "Two against one."

Before the man could answer, James barreled him into the wall and dropped him to the ground. James kneed him in the face as the man crumpled unconscious.

Panting, James addressed the sprawled bodies, "Next floor show in twenty minutes."

Bolles grinned. "Look at you."

James shrugged. "Two against two."

The two of them hurried away and made it back to James car. "How did you find me?"

"I've been keeping my eye on you, and you can bet others are too," Bolles responded.

"Why are you here?"

"I've heard you are seeking the truth, and the truth is, I know what it is."

James put the car in gear. "And?"

"I warned Chris—your mother—to stay away from town that night."

James questioned, "But you were there that night, at the Grand." He turned to catch Bolles's expression. "Why did you leave her?"

Bolles lowered his head. "I saved myself. It is the biggest regret of my life." Bolles continued. "It was a hit, straight up. They set up a gauntlet. There were separate teams planning and hoping for the jackpot. They stalked her until she fell into the—"

"Ambush." James slapped the steering wheel.

"The narrow bridge with the unprotected row of steel support beams provided the ideal conditions for the 'accident.'"

"Do you know why?"

Bolles sighed. "There was a problem." Then Bolles saw something that spooked him.

"What's wrong?"

"Let me off here." He waved his hand to the curb. "Here, now."

James pulled over and Bolles opened the door before the car came to a complete stop. As he exited, he said, "If Louis remarried while Christina was alive, in the eyes of church, he could never be king. But

he could take the throne if he were a widower. So problem solved."
Bolles stepped out of the car and looked back in. "It was Louis." With
that revelation, Bolles bolted from the car and disappeared into the
night.

James stared into the abyss of the darkest night.

Chapter 48

Lying in bed, James had a restless night staring at the ceiling. He had finally landed on that haunted shore.

Two different people had stated with certainty that two different members of his family had ordered the death of his mother. My family can't be made up of that much evil, can it? He rolled out of bed and made his way to the shower. For a half hour, he attempted to wash away the nightmare others had painted. When he finished, Warden waited for him in his room.

"How is the sink?"

Warden shook his head in disgust. "I had to resort to a professional."

"Good choice." He smiled. "You know, I need to get away for a while. I'm thinking about a drive to the ocean."

"If you want to go alone, that won't be possible today, James."

"Excuse me?"

"Malcolm had some sort of auto problems and came early this morning requesting your VW Rabbit. I assumed you would say yes, so I allowed him the privilege. He said he would bring it back by three."

"You mean to tell me with all the vehicles we have at the palace, he couldn't have picked one from there?"

"He said it was a private matter and didn't want anyone to know."

"Including me. Please arrange something for me today."

Warden helped James into his shirt. "You are the brother of a thousand secrets. I suspect he assumes you aren't running to your father to mention he took your car."

James huffed. "I suppose that's a fair assumption."

The penthouse phone rang, something that only happened when the royal house called.

Warden turned to James. "Are you expecting a call?"

"On that phone? Hardly."

Woom came into view. "Your Highness," a nervous pitch quivered in her voice, "your brother has been in an accident."

"Is he okay?"

"He's in the hospital."

James looked at Warden.

The three of them made their way down to the basement and alerted Vern and Rex of the situation. They hopped in Warden's car and the detail followed them to the emergency room. It was the same lonely corridor James walked the night his mother died.

Hospital security met them and escorted them to a private elevator and took them to the intensive care unit. On a floor designated only for the royal family, they met his father coming from his brother's room.

James swallowed his suspicions of his father long enough to ask, "How is he?"

"Come with me. I'm headed to see the doctor." Louis tried to put his arm around his son, but James backed away.

They walked down a long hallway to an open door. James felt as if he didn't know the man next to him.

Inside, a woman in scrubs with a stethoscope wrapped around her neck studied a series of X-rays. The room glowed of opaque lighting coming from images of a spine.

Prince Louis asked, "How is my son, doctor?"

She continued staring at the screens. "He's stable and is going to survive."

Louis continued. "Thank God."

"And with time and rehabilitation, there is no reason he can't lead a normal life."

James shuddered and stared at the screen, listening to the conversation.

Louis asked, "Normal life?"

"Your Highness, Prince Malcolm sustained permanent neural damage below the lumbar three vertebra." She turned and stared at the two of them with a dispassionate look.

Louis' eyes welled. "A paraplegic?"

She nodded. "I'm sorry, but your son is alive and will survive."

James left his father with the doctor and made his way back to Malcolm's room. Inside, a machine blipped and a hose made pumping sounds. A nurse checked Malcolm's vital signs.

When James came in, she took her leave. James leaned over his brother, Malcolm's eyes dark like a prizefighter who had lost.

"Malc, tell me you're okay."

A soft, groggy voice slurred, "I'm alive."

James leaned over. "Malc, what happened?"

He whispered, "Your damn Rabbit. I was driving out by the bluff and your car lost all the brakes." His eyes rolled. "Damn drugs. I can barely think."

"Just rest."

"James, I can't feel anything. Did I lose my legs?"

"Right now, it's important, that you rest."

Malcolm started to lift his hand but dropped it back down as he drifted back to sleep.

James turned to leave and the door flew open. The queen and Prince Richard stepped in with a fevered pitch of disgust. James stared back as he passed them.

Outside the room, Woom and Warden asked of Malcolm's condition.

"He's in bad shape, but they say he'll live."

James could see Woom was visibly upset. She always had a protective side toward Malcolm. He asked Warden, "Who knew he had asked to take my car?"

"I knew. He came and asked me."

James turned to Woom. "Did you know?"

"Of course."

James asked, "What about the detail. Did they know?"

Warden said, "Rex knew. He said he was on watch when Malcolm came out."

"Where was Vern?"

"He'd been up late and was sleeping."

James nodded, "Huh." He said to the pair, "If you want to stay you may, or you can go back to the penthouse. I have something to do."

Woom opted to stay while Warden agreed to return home and field any calls that might come in. Since it was James's car, there may be public uncertainty as to which royal member had been in an accident.

Warden and James left together, and in the lobby of the hospital, a shocked Alba collapsed into James's arms.

"I heard the news and thought it was you."

"I'm fine, but I have some questions."

Alba looked up. "For whom?"

He scanned the outer concourse of the hospital. "Rex."

Chapter 49

When the three of them made it out to the parking lot, James's detail was nowhere in sight. "I can't ever get rid of them, and now when I'm looking for them, I can't find them."

Alba asked, "What do you need them for?"

"Someone tampered with my car. I'm sure of it. Malcolm said the brakes weren't working. They live out there, and they see everyone who comes and goes. If something is more watched than me, it's my car." James paced, picked up his phone, and dialed his detail.

"Vern speaking."

"Where are you guys?"

"Coming."

James asked Alba, "Did you drive here?"

"Yes."

"Could you drive me back to the penthouse?"

"Of course."

Warden excused himself and went to fetch his car.

James's detail squealed around the corner, and when it pulled up alongside, James noticed Vern was alone.

Vern lowered the window, "Sorry, sir."

"Where is Rex?"

"Damnedest thing. When we got here, he said he needed to check on something, and he never returned."

"So where did you go?"

"I thought I saw him at the far end of the hospital grounds boarding a bus and I gave it a chase, but I lost it."

James felt irritated. "We need to find him."

Vern asked, "If I may ask, why?"

James mentioned, "Rex was on duty last night. Is that correct?"

"Yes, sir."

"Did you guys leave the garage?"

"I did. I came up and slept in my quarters. But Rex stayed in the garage until I replaced him."

James gritted his teeth. He knew the sabotaged car was meant for him, and now he knew which member of his detail had been part of the sabotage. "Just find him."

James turned to Vern. "Find him!"

Vern drove off while James waited for Alba.

James and Alba reconvened at the penthouse and James went over all the possibilities of who could have set this tragedy up. Who had an ax to grind with his family, to make them appear evil? "Who could be setting up my family?"

Alba settled in on the couch. "I think all roads lead to the truth, and I think you're denying the truth, James."

"That's what everyone wants me to believe, but I have to consider every possibility. It's my family so I have to be absolutely sure. Let's take the approach that maybe it's someone trying to divide and conquer my family."

Alba went quiet.

"Could this be corporate fed? The military? Maybe intelligence. Maybe someone in the government who wants to bring down the crown?"

Finally Alba asked, "James, can I apply some logic for a moment?"

"Please."

"If it had been anyone other than the royal family trying to neutralize your mother, wouldn't the obvious choice been to disgrace her by revealing the pregnancy? After all, your mother and father weren't divorced yet. She was killed because someone wanted her removed and forgotten. That's why after four years, no memorial to her has been erected."

As James ran his hand through his hair, tension welled up inside him. "Perhaps Richard, but my father would have fought him tooth and nail." Could power be that corrupt? Could greed be that invasive? "I have to exhaust all the possibilities."

Alba pulled away. "There are none. And whoever killed your mother is trying to kill you."

Suddenly James had an epiphany. "I got it. The cameras."

"What?"

"The surveillance cameras in the garage."

He took her hand and they moved to the elevator.

They made it to the ground floor and James hurried to the security room. He knocked and Mr. Powell, head of the building's security, shouted, "Who is it?"

"James."

The door opened. "Your Highness, to what do I owe the pleasure?"

"I need to view the tapes from last night."

Mr. Powell tilted his head and asked, "Which tapes?"

"The garage."

Powell stepped aside and allowed James and Alba to enter. "Right this way."

They made their way to a room with a dozen screens, all showing different locations around the building. Screen 4 showed an eerie empty bay where James car would have been. "Right there." James asked, "Can you roll it back?"

"How far?"

"Until you see activity."

Mr. Powell reversed the tape, speeding it through the hours until the car reappeared and Malcolm exited. The tape continued until a dark blip left the screen blank.

"Stop."

Powell hit pause.

"Keep going backward."

Powell ran it slowly backward until the camera appeared to tilt upward and the cars were visible again. "What the hell?" He scrolled slowly forward, watching until the image was twisted downward. Someone had repositioned the camera.

"What time was that?"

Powell checked the chronometer. "Looks like 3:52 a.m."

Alba whispered, "Vern said Rex was on duty."

James scowled. "I know." He told Powell, "Go back again until we see people."

As he did, they saw a neighbor, Lady Callahan, returning from somewhere. A half hour earlier, they saw a young couple, hands clutched together, enter the building. Around the midnight hour, the camera had a two-minute glitch. Nothing but snow.

"What happened there?"

Powell shrugged his shoulders. "I don't know." He checked the other cameras for that time. All twelve experienced the same glitch. "Interesting."

Alba asked, "What happened?"

Powell looked at James. "There's only one way they could have all gone out at once. Someone tampered with the central optic fiber. The only people who would have access to that, would be someone with high authority like ... your people."

The thought of Rex tampering with his car sent James into a fury. "Damn it."

Alba rubbed his arm. "You had no way of knowing."

"Maybe not, but I never trusted him."

James spent a couple of hours winding and rewinding the tapes, visiting every angle to try and pin anything down. It was clear the glitch hid something, but he wasn't sure what. He pulled out his phone and called Vern. "Anything on Rex?"

"Nothing. Not sure where he went."

James asked, "Do you know where Rex's parents live?"

"Already went there. They say they haven't seen him either."

"Okay, come back. It's probably wise that I have you with me now." He hated to admit it, but right now, having a bodyguard might come in handy. The fact that his family might be involved didn't escape the irony of the family-imposed protection.

James and Alba made their way back to the penthouse. Warden met them at the elevator.

"James, there's a new development."

James glanced at his servant. "What?"

"The police have found Rex."

"Where is that son of a bitch?"

"Well, I suppose right about now at the morgue."

James stared at Warden. "What?"

"He was found face down in the river this afternoon, apparently with a gunshot wound to his head. They say self-inflicted."

James asked Alba, "Do you think a hired gun would take himself out if he failed an assignment?"

Alba shrugged. "Beats me, but something tells me you don't think so."

"Warden, who was responsible for hiring Rex?"

"James, I wouldn't know that."

"Can you find out?"

Warden took a seat opposite the prince. "My relationship with you warrants little trust from the queen. I'm afraid I could not get close enough to employment records to get that information."

"Is there another option?"

"If you might indulge me for a moment, I'd like to suggest someone whom you have very little faith in."

The pair squared off silently and James lifted his shoulders. "Who?"

"Woom is still very trusted by the crown."

James laughed. "Of course she is. She tells them everything."

Unaware Woom had returned from the hospital, James stiffened when her voice boomed out from behind him. "My allegiance ends if my boys are in harm's way."

James turned and bowed in apology. "I didn't realize you were here."

"Be that as it may, your sentiments are understood."

James felt uncomfortable letting Woom into the inner circle that included Alba, Warden, Colin, and Vern. "Well, if Warden trusts you ..." James hesitated, gazing at the woman who'd helped raise him. "Hell, I can't believe you'd do me harm."

Woom smiled with mist in her eyes. "You and your brother are why I exist."

James's phone buzzed. "Vern is here." He pulled his phone out. "We're upstairs. Come up."

When the five of them collected in the front room, James gave Vern the news about Rex.

Vern towered over the group. "Damn. I can't believe Rex would do that."

"Why?" James responded.

"He just didn't strike me as covert. He said what he meant and didn't hide his feelings about anything."

James sighed. "Well, sometimes you never really know people you work with."

Vern popped a kink in his neck. "I guess not."

They sat around the table and James suggested, "Woom, you are going to have to get to the file room at the palace. I suspect the person responsible for my car is the person who hired Rex."

She cautioned him, "You are aware you are about to implicate a family member?"

James shrugged. "No, I'm implicating someone who tried to murder me, nearly killed my brother, and probably killed my mother." He turned to Vern. "I want you to escort her and make sure she stays in one piece."

Vern nodded.

"Alba and I," James turned to Warden, "and you are going to take a drive."

Warden asked, "To where?"

James grinned. "It doesn't matter." He lifted his phone and called Colin. "Mate, I need your assistance."

"James, I heard Malcolm was seriously hurt. Is he okay?"

"It's very bad. He won't be able to walk."

"That's terrible. I'm sorry to hear that."

"I need your help." James stood and walked toward the window, looking far below to the street. "I need you to follow us from a distance. I need to know if we are being tailed." James set up where Colin could start his tail then released Woom and Vern to the palace. "Be careful, you two. No telling who wants me dead. And remember everyone is suspect."

Vern responded, "I understand, Your Highness."

James escorted Vern and Woom to the elevator and gave Woom a hug. "I'm sorry for how I've treated you."

"I am at your service, Your Highness." Woom curtsied.

"James. I will always be James to you."

She touched his cheek. "You are so much like your mother."

James reached up and squeezed her fingers. "Thank you."

She and Vern went down the elevator.

When the elevator returned, Warden had everyone's coats. James joined Alba and Warden in the elevator. On the way down, the elevator stopped on the eighth floor and Lady Callahan stepped in.

James smiled. "You were out awfully late last night."

"Why, Prince James, are you stalking me? I'm flattered." She gazed at Alba, "And is my beauty taking your attention away from this lovely creature?"

Alba tipped her head. "Thank you."

Lady Callahan casually asked, "So did that man fix your car?"

James came around the side of the woman and bent forward. "What man?"

She exchanged glances with everyone in the elevator. "My goodness, you all looked shocked."

"Do you mean my bodyguard?"

"Well, yes, but he just watched. It was the mechanic who worked on your car."

"Did you talk to them?"

"Oh, heaven's no. I don't think they even knew I was there. I had dropped something by the door and came back for it. I only opened it for a second. They never saw me."

"That probably saved your life."

"You're joking."

"Listen carefully. Last night, you saw my bodyguard and another man at my car. You saw the muscular, dark-haired bodyguard."

"No, Your Highness. I saw the tall, blond fellow."

"What did the mechanic look like?"

"I don't recall, but he was older, had a limp, like a leg too short."

James recalled Vern's father, Mr. Farrell, was a high-end mechanic.

Alba blurted out, "Woom."

James hurried Warden. "Call her now."

Warden already had his phone in his hand. "On it." He growled. "It's going straight to voice mail." He tried again and again.

As James exited the elevator. "We're going to the palace."

Chapter 50

The sun settled in the west, a bright orange orb dropping below the hills.

Three miles from the palace, as they sped around the last bend, they stopped. Resting on the side of the road was Vern's car.

James ran to the car, but no one was inside.

A deep ravine to the right side of the road caught James's eyes. Then a head bobbed up as Woom stepped up onto the road. She waved her arms.

James slammed the door and hurried to her. "Are you okay?"

"I am."

"Where is Vern?"

She gestured toward the ravine. "He's probably still rolling to the bottom."

James looked down at a lifeless Vern. He turned back to Woom. "What the hell?"

"He was a bad egg, James."

"I see that, but no offense, he's two hundred and fifty pounds. You might weigh ninety-five soaking wet."

"One hundred on the nose, thank you."

"What happened?"

She pulled a handgun from her coat pocket. "He's not the only one trained to protect you boys."

Colin pulled up in his car. "Well, doesn't look like anyone is following you."

James realized he still held the element of surprise. "Colin, Warden, hell, Alba, we need to keep Vern on ice for a day or two."

Alba objected. "I'm not going down there to carry him up."

"You are going to have to. I think it will take us all."

Together they strained and grunted the mercenary up the hill. They packed him away in his trunk.

Colin asked, "So who's driving his car?"

James sighed. "Well, Warden is going to have to take Woom the rest of the way. So I guess that leaves me."

Alba rubbed his shoulder. "I'll ride shotgun with you."

James turned to Woom. "I hate to ask you to continue. We have no idea what Vern reported."

Woom winked. "I don't think he's reported a word. He was too busy telling me how I chose the wrong side."

James eyed Woom. You are one amazing woman.

Alba asked, "Why continue? We know it wasn't Rex."

"Two reasons," James surmised. "If Vern did get word out, someone is expecting Woom to show up. I want to know who specifically hired Vern. I can't accuse all my family if only one member is guilty." James turned to Woom. "Did Vern say who he worked for?"

"He did not, and I thought shooting him was better than negotiating. Sorry, James."

"You're fantastic!" exclaimed James.

James had misread everyone close to him. He had accused Alba of being a traitor, Woom of being a loyalist, and Vern of being his bodyguard. He miscalculated them all. He stared at Warden and Colin. "Life is a humbling experience."

Warden stared back. "James, are you okay?"

Colin smirked. "Old boy is sizing us up, Warden." He pulled up alongside James. "You needn't worry about me. You've cost me a bookstore and my wife is always upset that you will get me in trouble.

Believe me, if I haven't killed you yet, chances are you're safe with me."
He cleared a path between James and his butler.

James sighed. "If I really thought either of you two were my en-
emies, I'd just give up this fight. I have to rely on you. I've come to
believe in you all."

Warden dismissed James. "Well, you don't have much choice at
this point. As Colin has pointed out, opportunity has presented itself
every day of my life since I feed you."

"If Mum were here, she'd say, 'I was so much older then. I'm
younger than that now.'" James winked.

Then everyone divided up and headed toward their cars.

Woom stepped up to give James a peck on the cheek. "Be careful."

James nodded his head. "You be careful." He nodded to Warden.
"You too."

Colin and Alba waited as James stood alongside the road and
watched Warden drive Woom into enemy territory.

Chapter 51

Woom's mission had been a disappointment. Any mention of who had actually interviewed Vern was scrubbed from his file. In fact, his record had been heavily redacted and blacked out.

James still had options. With the five of them back together at the penthouse, James offered, "Vern's father was in on this. Let's go pay him a visit."

Alba objected. "James, this is no longer safe. We need to involve the police."

James scoffed. "The police? Seriously? There is no reason to believe the police wouldn't go straight to whoever in my family is responsible. That would make this more dangerous than it already is." He put his arm around Alba. "Besides, I have someone else we can send."

Colin piped up. "Who?"

"Don't forget Mr. Hassan has quite the marketing team." James pulled his phone out and started to place a call.

"James!" Warden put his finger to his lips and silenced his royal charge.

James disconnected and the room hushed in silence.

Warden held something up. It appeared to be a small listening device.

James studied it and whispered, "Where did you find that?"

Warden walked him into the kitchen and pointed to the sink.

James grabbed a notepad and jotted down, "Plumber?"

Warden nodded.

James scribbled on the notepad, "The room is bugged," and circulated it to the rest of the team. James played up to the chances someone was listening. "On second thought, leave Al Hassan out of this. He's refused to work with us. He wants to be left alone." James craned his neck and looked under the shade of a lamp. "Alba's right. We should just call the police and let them take care of it." James held his hands up as Alba's mouth fell open.

James scribbled back. "To Plato's Cave."

Colin laughed. Everyone picked up their coats and headed for the elevator.

When they made it to the street and walked into Plato's Cave Coffee Shop, drawing the attention of the local citizenry.

Alba said, "I seriously hope the front room isn't bugged. If it is, they know Vern's dead."

Warden mused, "I don't think us confirming it did any more than what they must already suspect. Vern had to be checking in regularly. They have to be wondering where he is."

"Still, dead is not missing. It's dead." Colin asked, "So what's next?"

James directed. "First, you need to get your wife and go on vacation. I don't want to be responsible for losing you." He turned to Woom. "That goes for you too."

Woom frowned, snapping the top button of her jacket against the brisk chill of the wind. "I'm not going anywhere."

"You know what happened to Malcolm. This is a perilous path we're on." James noticed the same confidence she had when he and his brother were little. When she expected her words to be followed. He wouldn't win this battle. "Very well, but we all need to know where we all are at all times."

Alba grinned. "I guess that means I should stay with you, huh?"

As James grabbed her hand and they crossed the street, a paparazzo snapped a photo. "Well, there's a love interest photo for the paper."

Colin added, "Or the new gang of five," referring to their motley crew.

James pulled out his cell phone again. "Well, it's about to grow." He placed a call to Al Hassan and discussed his security team paying a visit to Vern's parents. They agreed to meet at the Aurora Bridge by the coast after Hassan's men had picked up the mechanic.

Colin separated and bid the others good luck. He'd be taking the wife on a trip out of town.

"Be careful. Until you are safely tucked away, don't take any chances." James feared for his friend. Everyone in his party was a means of getting James to quit his quest.

Chapter 52

James expected Al Hassan to come with Vern's father, so his arrival alone concerned him. As Al Hassan stepped out of his car, the look on his face expressed failure.

"What happened?" James leaned against his car while Alba sat inside.

Mr. Hassan glanced around. A few fishermen dotted the water below the Aurora Bridge. "Your man, Vern's father, is dead."

"You killed him?"

Hassan waved his hands. "No, absolutely not. James, I wish you would quit thinking I operate that way."

"Then how?"

"We arrived to a house ablaze and two bodies being removed."

James shook his head.

"James, I'm a man who lost a son. You are a man who lost a mother. The more you dig, the more you may lose." He stepped closer and put an arm on James's shoulder. "I'm with you in any way I can be, but things are no longer safe."

"So are you bailing on me?"

"I suggest you let the dust settle a year, perhaps two, then restart this. Right now, we only put ourselves in a position where we will join our loved ones."

James nodded. "I understand. However, I'm done waiting."

Mr. Hassan bowed. "Very well." He backed away and returned to his vehicle.

James watched as he pulled away and raced off.

Alba lowered the window. "What did he say?"

"We're all alone."

Chapter 53

The next day came with an urgent call from the hospital. Malcolm had awakened and wanted to speak with James. He hadn't requested any other family, just James.

Alba had taken a guest room and the call came while the four of them sat for breakfast. They hurried to the intensive care unit of the hospital.

James entered Malcolm's room alone. "Hey Malc, how are you feeling?"

Malcolm's eyes trembled, his face swollen and bruised. In a drug-induced voice, he said, "Besides pissing in a bag and a disabled Willie, everything's perfecto." He fumbled with the knob of a radio and turned it up. He motioned James to come closer and whispered, "I want the truth."

James focused. "The truth?"

Malcolm sighed. "I want the fucking truth. If I knew it, I wouldn't be here."

"I know, but right now you need to rest and rehab. I'll get to the truth, I promise you."

Malcolm pointed his finger; tubes draped off him like a marionette. "God damn it! This was meant for you." He motioned toward his legs. "My guess is because of your snooping about mum."

"I'm sorry I did this to you."

Malcolm stared through slit eyelids. "You did not do this bullshit to me."

"I promise you I'll get to the bottom of this, and I will make sure you are the first to know." He reached down and put his hand on his brother's shoulder. "But right now, I need to ask you something."

Malcolm ran his palms over his face and rubbed his temple. "What do you want from me? What can I do?" His voice cracked as a tear swept down his cheek.

"You're the only one I can trust."

Malcolm laughed; an absurd expression lit up his face. "Then you have a real fucking problem."

James remained serious. "Listen." he gripped Malcolm's chin and forced him to make contact. "If anything—anything—happens to me, like suicide, whether by overdose, drowning, gunshot, or—"

"Or accident." Malcolm spit the words out.

"Don't let them sweep it under the rug. Remember Mum taught us to make a difference."

Malcolm stared, a cold anger behind blue eyes. "We're fucking orphans."

James leaned over. "I'm so sorry this happened. I will make it right."

Tears streamed out of Malcolm's eyes as he waved James away.

Chapter 54

James was engrossed at his desk, pouring over the files and transcripts, barely interrupted by swallows of coffee.

Tense and exhausted, Alba whispered, "I'm done, James."

"Just a bit more and then we'll get something to eat."

"No, I'm resigning. I can't do this anymore."

James looked at her.

Alba remained silent.

"Let the chips fly."

"Can I be honest with you?"

"I hope you are always honest with me."

"If you carry out your plan tomorrow, you'll be killed. They won't stop."

"You know I can't stop."

She looked at him with fear and resolve. "Sorry, I'm a coward."

James shook his head.

"Aren't you afraid?"

"Of course. But I have a responsibility."

Her eyes filled with tears as he placed his hand on her arm. "Look at your brother; that could be you."

James concentrated. "That is me. It's me to the core. And I can't let it rest."

"I'm afraid if you uncover this, it will be everything you know that's against you. Then they will kill you."

"You know I can't stop. The trail leads to my own family. Someone in my family murdered my mother. But everything we've uncovered is circumstantial. Vern worked for my family and put my brother in a hospital. He didn't do that on his own. He was ordered."

Alba bowed her head. "The next step is yours, and I'm worried about that step because I think—"

James touched her chin raising her head and whispered, "Alba, life is wrong and hopeful … and tragic and courageous …"

"I can't help it. I tried not to care, but I—"

James put a finger to her lips to stop her. "You know, you've never told me what 'Alba' means?"

"'Alba'? It's Spanish for sunrise. Morning light."

"Morning light?" James remembered his mother's last words to him.

"My mother and father met someone named Alba. They just fell in love with it."

"I know." He kissed her passionately.

They made love for the first time.

Chapter 55

Ostentatious and inspiring, St. William Cathedral had held every royal wedding for five hundred years.

James arrived fashionably late and worked his way to the front of the ceremony.

Two hands were joined together.

A gray-haired priest, looking more at home in a kitchen than a pulpit, called out, "Do you, Louis, take Gardenia for your lawfully wedded wife?"

Prince Louis had the look of a man enjoying a rare moment of comfort. "I do." His eyes stared at James's future stepmother.

The priest concluded, "I now pronounce you man and wife." He checked his watch and declared, "The whole rehearsal timed in at thirteen minutes."

Louis sparked to life, ready to abandon the formalities. "Well done. That seems to work." He turned to his bride-to-be. "Gardenia, what do you think?"

A matronly woman, middle aged, nothing striking, dull brown hair, average brown eyes, and cheekbones softened by a few pounds, she offered, "Wonderful. Beautiful."

James didn't dislike Gardenia; he just didn't care for the substitute nature of her existence.

The cast of this rehearsal, the entire batch of best men and maids of honor, streamed down the steps of the stage. The women lifted their dresses and the men acted as though the event surrounded them.

James wondered how pompous it would be when they had on their full regalia of gowns and suits.

Louis gained everyone's attention. "Please, everyone, join us at the rehearsal dinner, and absolutely bring your appetite."

Prince Richard passed James, who stood to greet him. "Are you planning on being late for the wedding as well?"

"That depends on if I'm allowed to bring who I want."

He squared off with James. "No one is going to say anything about you bringing that Oriental girl."

"Her name is Alba, Grandfather."

"Be that as it may, the issue is her religion. You are the future heir to the throne, and she is, after all, a Buddhist." He paused with a grin. "You are aware she can be nothing more than a fancy. Have your way with her, but remember to discard her when you are done."

James controlled his temper. He wanted to thump the old man, but enough blood had been spilled. Besides, the spectacle he planned to engage in wouldn't be here.

"I hope to see you at the dinner."

"I won't miss it, Grandfather."

James worked his way out of the cathedral and into a waiting car. Warden reduced to his chauffeur and Woom, the shotgun assistance. "I do believe we have a dinner to attend to."

He tapped Woom. "Is Alba in place?"

"She is at the hospital with the camera and computer." She handed James a laptop opened to an image of Malcolm waving.

"Hey, Malc, how's it going?"

"I think for the first time since the accident, things are going better for me than for you." Malcolm grinned and James felt a burden lift.

"Good to see you in such good spirits at my expense."

"Oh, it's not at your expense. It's because I'm here with this incredible woman."

Alba stepped on the other side of the camera and waved. "Love you."

James, Woom, and Warden made their way to the palace and parked.

Warden turned to James. "I'm going to remain here, just to make sure the car remains untouched."

James laughed. "There are enough camera-wielding paparazzi to rival an American tourist bus. I'd say we are safe."

"Still."

James bowed. "Suit yourself." James turned to Woom said, "Keep Warden safe."

James gathered the computer and said to his brother. "Very well. I guess you and I are going in stag."

Chapter 56

The palace servants greeted James and placed him at one end of the dining table. Big enough to seat four to an end. The queen occupied one end by herself, Richard on the elbow to her left. James sat beside Gardenia, who sat beside her Louis.

To James's left, he waved off interested seat takers from the odd empty seat. He placed the laptop in front of him and pointed his brother's image onto the future newlyweds.

Louis cheered. "Here! Here! My youngest boy attends as well." He took the laptop and held it high, turning the screen for everyone to see." He smiled at James. "A splendid idea. I applaud you." He raised his glass and clinked champagne to Gardenia's outstretched glass.

Gardenia, in her innocence, smiled. "James, please sit with us. I rarely get to speak with you." The servants began the process of ladling out gluttonous helpings of food. "I hope you enjoy the food. I personally selected it."

James remained quietly composed, the thin smile never leaving his face.

Someone from the gallery of guests shouted, "Prince James, what deb did you bring?" while pointing at the empty chair beside him.

"Well," James said as he raised his glass and stood behind a row of guests, "I brought the only woman I could think of: my mother."

A wave of nervous laughter rippled through the crowd. James

embellished. "What do you give a man who has everything?" He
gestured to his father.

Someone shouted, "A small island!" The crowd roared.

"How about the truth?" He glanced at Gardenia. "I decided to
bring the truth."

Another guest asked, "What truth?"

There was no turning back. James viewed the screen of his brother
nodding him on. "The truth about my mother's death."

The crowd turned tense. The festive air sucked from the room.

"My mother left this house to get away from the crown and from
my father." He turned to Gardenia. "And I hope you don't wish the
same thing someday."

With his champagne glass held out like a sword, James targeted
his family. "She couldn't avoid the press. The paparazzi loved her,
her beauty, her compassion, and her sincerity. She met a man, Ali
Hassan. They fell in love, and together they played cat and mouse
with the press. My mother and Ali Hassan spent their last night alive
shadowed and harassed by the paparazzi."

Richard stood. "We've heard the account of that night. Sit down.
This is your father's night."

"No, I will not, and you will listen. I am the future king and these
people have the right to hear this." He turned to his father and motioned him to stay put. He continued. "My mother found herself at
the Grand Hotel, surrounded by the press, but secured by bodyguards
and hotel workers. But this is what you don't know."

Every eye followed James and every ear listened.

"My mother was making plans on leaving my father because she
was pregnant."

The crowd erupted in whispers.

"Enough!" The queen banged her spoon against her glass. The
noise softened when the glass shattered.

The room went silent.

Then Malcolm's voice crackled from the computer. "I want to
hear more."

James pointed to Malcolm and shrugged his shoulders. James gathered himself. "They had dinner in the penthouse suite, but instead of spending the night there, Ali Hassan wanted to return to his apartment where a 300,000-euro engagement ring awaited them. Where," James emphatically charged, "he would propose to marry her when she was free of this house."

James turned to his father, who shook his head in disappointment. For his part, his father neither scolded him nor prevented him from continuing.

"Cromwell Clay-Bauer, the head of hotel security, in order to deceive the paparazzi, proposed sending bodyguards from the front as a decoy while they exited from the rear. Because this action would separate the bodyguard's car from Ali Hassan and Mother, the bodyguard, Clare Thornton-Smith strongly protested."

James snapped a finger to a servant holding champagne. He recharged his glass and continued.

"But Ali overruled her. So just after midnight, the plan was set in motion as the decoy convoy departed from the front. At 12:15 a.m., they boarded an SUV parked behind the hotel. Though not licensed to be a chauffeur, Clay-Bauer drove on their ill-fated trip. But this particular SUV had an unusual history."

The audience remained captivated, but the queen had had enough. She might not be able to stop her grandson from revealing every sordid detail, but she refused to listen. Gathering herself, she left the table, whispering something to Richard as she left.

James singled her out. "Grandmother, don't you wish to hear the rest?"

"Oh go ..." She waved her hand and stopped her thought.

"As I was saying, four weeks earlier, the SUV was stolen by three armed men. Two weeks later, it turned up with its EMS or Electronic Management System ripped out. The EMS controls the steering and the brakes. But the EMS has no resale value. A new system was installed, and the car was returned to the hotel."

"Not fooled by the decoy, the paparazzi were waiting as Clay-Bauer drove around the front of the hotel. But instead of taking the most direct route to Ali's apartment, Clay-Bauer took the route along the river." James held a finger high. "Why did he take this route? Did the 5,000 in cash found on him make him have another agenda?" James looked at the remaining family at the table. "Another master?"

"They were hunted by a horde of paparazzi on scooters as well as a dark sedan and a high-powered motorcycle with two riders. At the river, Clay-Bauer jumped the red light, hitting speeds up to 100 miles per hour, leaving the paparazzi far behind. But the dark sedan and the motorcycle continued stalking them."

"The white sedan came to a standstill on the right side of the entrance to the Old Boston Bridge. Because of the row of unprotected support beams dividing the bridge, the conditions were perfect. It was a well-coordinated, professional operation."

"The motorcycle driver radioed ahead, telling the white sedan to get ready. As Mother's SUV sped toward the bridge entrance, there waited the sedan. When the SUV got to the bridge, the sedan picked up speed. At the same moment, the high-powered motorcycle with two riders passed the SUV on its left. Then the white sedan darted to the left in front of the SUV. Clay-Bauer swerved sharply to avoid colliding with the sedan but clipped the sedan's left tail light."

James moved around the table, drawing the audience with him as he spoke. When he made it to the queen's seat, he picked up a piece of broken glass and held it up. "The glass fragments from the white sedan's tail light were later found at the scene."

"Clare Thornton-Smith said she told everyone to buckle up but no one did … except her. My mother always wore her seatbelt, but not this night. Why? Because the rear seatbelts were useless. They could not be retracted."

"At that moment, the motorcycle moved directly in front of the SUV. Its passenger turned back and ignited an antipersonnel flash at Clay-Bauer. Its intensity would blind him for up to three minutes."

"Then two explosions were heard on the bridge. We know the second was the car's impact with the steel support beam, but what was the first explosion?" James dropped the glass and looked at Malcolm, who avidly followed James's timeline. "It was a small explosive planted in the EMS to dismantle the steering and brake systems. Triggered remotely, now it was impossible to control the car." He again looked at Malcolm and stated, "Sort of like my car."

"With the SUV gravely disabled, the white sedan accelerated, getting right next to the SUV. The white paint scrapings all along the SUV's right side are proof that the sedan had a second collision with the SUV, forcing it to the left. Pushing the SUV until it collided head-on with the thirteenth support beam."

Standing still, James sighed. "It was 12:23 a.m. The dark sedan drove by and assessed the wreck. It determined that Ali Hassan and Clay-Bauer were killed instantly but my mother was still alive. So the backup plan was activated."

"At 12:27 a.m., a passing doctor, Dr. John Sartine, stopped and attended the injured. He said mother was conscious. Mother said, 'My God, what happened? Is everyone okay?' She also told the doctor she was pregnant. Dr. Sartine felt hers was not a catastrophic injury."

"At 12:40 a.m., two ambulances arrived with doctors on board. The patient care passed from Dr. Sartine to the ambulance doctor, Dr. Marengo. At 1:00 a.m., mother is removed from the SUV and transferred into the ambulance. Ali Hassan and Clay-Bauer were declared dead at the scene."

"Mother's depressed blood pressure and rapid heart rate were signs of internal bleeding. Getting her to an emergency room ASAP was critical." James shook his head in curiosity. "Yet Dr. Marengo continued to treat her on the bridge for forty minutes."

"Finally at 1:40 a.m., the ambulance left the bridge. Its destination was a hospital three miles away. But instead of speeding to the hospital, the convoy crawled at five miles per hour. They said 'to prevent further trauma.' Mother's vital signs continued to deteriorate. Then half a mile from the hospital, the ambulance stopped for ten minutes."

"Government officials waiting for Mother's arrival became concerned that the ambulance had somehow gotten lost."

"At 2:29 a.m., she arrived at the ER. To cover the three miles took forty-nine minutes. A tear in the superior vena cava blood vessel can be repaired, but time is critical. The emergency doctors worked frantically to save her, but it was too late. The total time of one hundred and nine minutes, nearly two hours, to get her from the crash to the hospital was fatal. Mother was declared dead. It was 3:22 a.m. Who was behind these killings?"

The audience along with Richard and Louis sat stone-faced. A tearful Malcolm wept, devastated by the revelations. The queen was nowhere to be found.

James found the chaos to be an accomplice to his quick escape. He gathered up the computer. As he turned, he caught Gardenia's face, flushed and somewhere between disappointment and disbelief. How much ire she directed at James and how much she directed at the royal family, he didn't know, but his speech had some sort of effect. He gave her an apologetic nod and moved around her.

He hurried down the steps, unsure what response would be directed at him. James joined Warden and Woom inside the car.

"Do you think the culprit will surface?" asked Warden.

"I hope so, or I've just made the biggest ass of myself in royal history. And with my family's past, that's saying something."

"I'm feeling less safe by the moment."

"Now I realize why truth and courage are revered across all cultures and borders. Because they are so rare."

Then James ordered Warden, "Floor it."

Chapter 57

When they made it back to the garage, Warden asked, "What about the car?"

James shrugged. "We're covered." James rapped on the adjacent parked car and two people raised their heads. Inside a dark tinted sedan, two of Al Hassan's men gave the thumbs-up.

Warden asked, "I thought Mr. Hassan was opting out."

James smiled. "Don't believe everything you hear."

"So is this our new detail?"

"For a moment."

When they made it to the penthouse, Alba met them at the elevator, grabbing James in a tight embrace.

James smiled. "You made it back mighty quick."

"I wanted to be here for you, I was so worried."

The hour struck midnight and Woom retired for the evening.

Warden suggested James and Alba do the same. He'd turned back the bedding in the guest room for Alba.

As she walked down the hall with James, he pulled her along as they passed her door, continuing on to his room. "I want to spend tonight with you."

Alba rested her head on his arm. "I thought you'd never ask."

He closed the door with a gentle click and quietly turned the lock.

A knock on James's door came early
"What is it?" James shouted. "It's six."
A muffled Warden answered, "Phone. Your father."
James nudged Alba, who gathered the sheet to cover her naked body. He kissed her and whispered, "My father wishes to speak to me."
"Interesting. Don't agree to anything."
James stood, pulled a robe from his bedside, and made his way to the room phone. "Yes, Father?"
"Something's happened, James."
James worried for his brother. Why else, after the performance from the night before, would his father care to tell him anything? "What is it?" His anxiety rose.
"Kerry Bolles was in a motorcycle collision on the turnpike last night."
Forgetting that there were no accidents anymore, James blurted, "My God, is he all right?"
"Fatal, I must say. It was an unfortunate accident, indeed." He paused. "I was sure you'd like to know. Good fellow and all. Had a rough spot, but … sad news." The phone went dead.
He walked back to the bed and disrobed. Alba's gaze concentrated on him. She opened the sheet and he slipped in with her. They clung together flesh to flesh. "Bolles has been killed." He stroked her raven hair, a contrast against the white sheets. "Must I be a part of this family?"
She swung a leg over him and pushed him onto his back. She slid over the top and rested her chest against his.
He reached up and pulled her toward him, and they embraced in passion. A half hour, an hour, maybe two went by before they released each other, out of breath, sweat drawing beads between them.
As they lay there, Alba smiled. "What did you dream about last night?"
He looked away and surmised, "Well, let's see. I confronted someone who's a killer and I made love to a woman."
"But what about your dreams?" She rested her chin on her palm and looked down into James's face.
"I dreamt that I was anonymous."

She rubbed his cheek and asked, "Anonymous how?"

"Completely unknown with only a passport and a toothbrush."

She gasped. "Where was I?"

"I was coming to see you."

"Good answer." She started to kiss him, but a knock from Warden interrupted again.

"Yes?" James winked and whispered, "Hold that thought."

"Phone again. This time, it's your grandfather."

"Okay!" he shouted back. "I wonder what this one wants to tell me?" He slid Alba off and lamented, "Duty calls. Sorry, sweetheart."

She sighed as he walked to the phone naked.

He winked as he answered, "Hello."

"Good morning, James. Something regarding your mother turned up in the family's depository. Compelling documents."

James began to wonder if the night before had been a dream. Everyone seemed to be dismissing his rather accusatory speech. He shrugged to Alba in disbelief. "What exactly are they?"

Prince Richard said, "It's better if you see them."

James didn't like the idea of trusting anything royal. As benign as his grandfather's tone was, until he knew the culprit, everyone was suspect. "Can you send them over?"

"James, quit being suspicious." His voice cracked. "I know you believe someone purposely did something to your mother, but I'm your grandfather. I adored your mother. At least give me the chance to side with you for a moment. If anyone in this family did anything to Christina, I will personally help you."

James exhaled an unsure breath. "Okay, what time?"

"Let's make it, say, six at the depository."

James hung up. He stood at his penthouse window and looked down at the city teeming with life.

Alba gathered the sheet into a toga and approached him. "What did he want?"

"He wants to solve a problem." He continued studying the masses below him. Duties, purposes, and lives he wished he had.

Alba wrapped her arms around him, her head rested into his back. "Please don't go. You're walking into their trap ..."

James felt sure. "Don't worry. I have both of you watching over me."

"Both?"

"You and Mother."

Warden knocked a third time. Alba laughed. "That man suspects we are up to some hanky-panky!"

James released Alba and grabbed his robe. He went to the door and unlocked it. Face-to-face with Warden, he said, "You have a key, and it's never stopped you from coming in before."

Warden whispered in a polite voice, "Well, the young lady wasn't in her room and I suspected she might be here. I thought it best not to disturb you."

"Thank you for the consideration, Warden. Now, is there another phone call?"

"No, James. Someone is waiting for you."

"Who?"

"Mr. Saxby Colberg, the queen's chief advisor."

James stood, puzzled over why the palace's "man in gray" was calling. The infamous family fixer and hatchet man.

"Why in the world would Colberg be here? Is anyone with him?"

"No, James. He's come alone."

"Be with you in a minute, Warden."

If Colberg was the problem-solver, then James was his problem.

James went over to Alba's purse. "I need to borrow something." He withdrew her Glock 9mm pistol then secreted it into the pocket of his robe.

Alba scrambled out of bed. "Wait a second." She took the pistol from his pocket and pulled back then released the breech with a metallic click, chambering a bullet. She handed the pistol back to James. "Be very careful."

Warden and James moved down the hall.

As James came around the corner to the front room, Saxby Colberg stood with his hat tucked in the wedge of his arm.

"Good morning, Saxby." James kept a firm grip on the pistol.

"Good morning, Your Highness." He fidgeted. A worried gaze on his brow.

"What can I do for you?"

Saxby looked uneasily at Warden. "Warden, can you leave us alone for a moment?"

Warden stiffened and stared at Colberg.

"It's okay, Warden. I have the situation under control," said James.

"Very well." He turned and made a quick line to the kitchen.

When they were alone, James asked, "Now, what is it?"

"I heard your speech last night."

James questioned, "Do you think it was a grave error?"

"Perhaps, but everyone from the palace caught the majority of your speech." He nodded. "News travels fast."

"And what brings you here?"

He stepped forward. "I've worked for the royal family for many years, and recently, I may have overheard some confidential conversations."

"Is that possible?"

"Well, let's just say I might have set up a listening device or two to verify what I suspected was being said."

"And?"

Colberg removed a cassette recorder from his pocket and placed it in James's hand. "Prince Richard is the one to fear. You must neutralize him. With this tape, you can win."

James twisted the cassette, viewing it like a puzzle. It was labeled, "Books on Tape."

"Why are you doing this?"

Colberg shrugged. "I'm a realist. The queen's old and Louis is weak. I'm betting youth will prevail." Colberg turned as quickly as he came and headed back to the elevator. Reaching the foyer, he stopped and faced James. "Remember who gave this to you, Your Highness. Long live the king."

James turned on the radio, then unearthed this treasure. On that tape, James heard the voices of the queen, Prince Richard, and his father. A back seat discussion with the queen leading the way. She ordered the group, his father weakly agreeing, and Richard the strong arm willing to carry out her dictates.

James listened, mesmerized by how easily they could treat family like hunted prey. Pure sangfroid.

He realized the enemy meant something different to them. It meant loss of power.

Alba, Woom, and Warden gathered as the four of them listened in total disbelief.

Alba chimed. "Well, clearly you can't go tonight."

Warden seconded that, and Woom nodded in agreement.

"No, I will."

Warden protested. "James, of all the harebrained things to do. Why would you walk into a trap?"

"I'll take protection." He eyed the two women. "You two aren't the only one with arms." He smiled. "Besides, I have the element of surprise."

Warden asked, "And what is that?"

"He doesn't know I know."

Alba teared up. "You aren't turning back, are you?"

He stood and addressed them all, whispering out of range of any listening device. "If I don't face this now, then the element of surprise is in their hands. I could be walking down the street one day and a stray bullet could find me. I'm not going down that way. One way or another, I'm facing my enemy."

Chapter 58

James prepared for his rendezvous by strapping Alba's Glock holster under his arm. He donned a loose jacket to conceal the weapon. He turned to see Woom and Alba hovering over him. "You two are making me nervous."

Woom was grim. "I can't stop worrying. I've held you for twenty-one years. I will never stop worrying."

He shook his head and pecked Woom on the cheek, turned to Alba, and gave her a kiss on the lips. "I'll see you later, promise."

He stepped toward the elevator, the room still quiet from the fear of bugs. He winked at Warden, waiting at the elevator door with his overcoat.

Warden played the role. "I hope Prince Richard has good information."

James whispered, "You better hope it isn't bugged. Colberg is pretty much dead if it is."

"I guess we'll find out."

James shook Warden's hand. "Take care of those two." He motioned to Alba and Woom who'd followed him into the foyer.

"I think Woom will be taking care of us." He winked at James.

James left early. If it was a trap, he suspected, Richard would treat James like the tardy fellow he'd always been. Richard wouldn't be prepared for an early bird.

At 4:30, he came within a mile of the Albion Depository and

parked his car off the side of the road. It was well concealed from view. He worked his way through the field and came up to the depository building. Quiet, undisturbed, with no one around.

He keyed the door with his pass and entered. The guard was gone. James wondered if Richard had dismissed him for the day for nefarious reasons. No matter. He'd come this far; he'd go the rest of the way. His heart beat rapidly and he patted the gun to quell his fear. When he came to rear chamber, he hit the doorplate and the door opened electrically. He hurried through and scanned the area. Dim lighting came from the ceiling lamps. Along with the filtered skylight, it created ghostly shadows and gave James an eerie feeling of not being alone.

James grabbed a chair and carried it to a row a few aisles from the door. He shoved aside the crates on the shelves. It gave him a hidden view of the only entrance.

Looking down, James nervously stretched and clenched his fingers.

As though his mother whispered to him, he felt calm waiting. His eyes shuddered. They snapped open, stirred by the sound of the door.

There was Prince Richard. Alone. He stood on the carpeted entryway, viewing the electric door, cursing something.

James watched as Richard studied the aluminum doorframe.

What are you up to?

Richard pulled something from his pocket and started rubbing the wiring on the side of the doorframe.

James squinted.

Richard continued scratching the surface. It was sandpaper.

After a minute, James could see the exposed wires. Now the hot wire would short circuit the electricity directly to the door's metal frame. James realized this was to be his death. Ambush by electrocution.

Richard gave it a final test. He hit the automatic doorplate. The door remained closed. Then Richard touched the doorframe.

James smiled as Richard jumped backward like he was on fire.

When Richard had finished, he walked over to the water cooler.

James held his chest, hoping to quiet his heartbeat.

Richard removed the glass canister and lugged it over to the doorway. Overkill.

Richard soaked the carpet to ensure the electric current would coarse from the wet carpet through James's body.

James shook his head. It figured. Richard would waltz in, set the ambush, and leave.

But then Richard stopped. He snapped his head to the right as though he heard something.

James remained as still as a dormouse.

Richard screamed, "Damn you, Christina!"

James watched as his frightened grandfather dropped the bottle. It shattered into large shards of glass. Water drenched his shoes. He acted disoriented, swinging his arms as though warding something away. "You can't be here. You're dead, Christina. Impossible."

James stood, came around the row, and revealed himself. "Grandfather?"

Richard looked at James in horror. Backing up and holding his hand up, "No, no, no. Stop."

James watched as his grandfather staggered and stumbled backward against the doorplate. It triggered the connection. Electricity flowed from doorframe to the wet rug and coursed throughout Richard's body.

James stared in dismay as his grandfather glowed and convulsed like an epileptic. The electricity exploded out his fingertips. Then Richard collapsed forward, his chest impaling on a shard of glass that pierced his chest and exited his back. Blood mixed with water.

The place went dark. By the soft light from the windows, he came up to Prince Richard, a smoldering smell of ozone about him. "Grandfather?"

James knelt and puts a finger to Richard's throat. Pushed in to feel a carotid pulse. Nothing. Grandfather had expired.

James scanned the room. "Mum, is that you?" He turned back to Richard. "She's watching over me. Didn't you know that?"

He stood over his grandfather and pushed the door open. He needed to leave before someone realized the power was out and came to fix it. No need for two royals to die that day.

Chapter 59

Driving, James was a man with a country, but not a family. And the family he belonged to was that country. He had become anonymous.

His resolve didn't come from him. It came from something deeper. From someone who still existed in his heart.

He pulled his phone out and punched the numbers to the palace.

The queen answered. "James, I saw your number pop up. I'm quite surprised."

"Grandmother, I'm sure you are very surprised."

"What's that supposed to mean, young man?"

"Well, you can imagine my meeting with Richard didn't go quite as you had hoped."

"James, you have me at a disadvantage. I'm at a loss as to what you are talking about."

"Well, Grandfather has expired and I had nothing to do with it." The silence led James to ask, "You still there, Grandmother?"

"I am. Please go on."

"Well as a matter of fact, I wanted you to be the first to hear the news before I go to the newspapers." James heard a gurgle. "Grandmother?" James heard a shriek from a chambermaid, followed by the voice of a young woman.

"Who is this?"

"This is James."

"Something has happened to the queen. She is pale and shaking."

James suggested. "Call an ambulance." He disconnected and floored the gas pedal.

When he made it back to the penthouse, he fell into the arms of Alba and whispered, "Mum really was with me."

Alba smiled. "I believe she was."

He turned to Warden. "Something's happened to Grandmother."

James explained what happened. His three housemates listened in stunned silence.

The penthouse went into full action mode.

Warden called to get the skinny on Prince Richard's sudden demise. It was already being spun as an accidental death. Then how that tragic news had triggered the queen's stroke.

James had one more person who had to be dealt with. He gathered Alba, Woom, and Warden and said, "I have one last trip to make."

Woom smiled. "Are you visiting the queen?"

James smiled, nodding in agreement.

Chapter 60

James used his royal authority to pass the royal guards. "Tell me, is my father with the queen?"

The captain nodded. "Third floor."

"I need you to give this envelope to Prince Malcolm." He handed the captain an envelope with an official seal.

"Yes, Your Highness." He saluted James.

James took the elevator to the third floor and casually walked to the nurse's station. "Where is my grandmother?"

A pretty, young nurse smiled. Her eyes lit up seeing Prince James. "Room 322."

"Thank you." He pushed off and worked his way past the guards securing the hall. When he made it to her room, he opened the door slightly, catching a glimpse of his father and his bride-to-be, Gardenia, hovering over his grandmother.

The queen was propped up, an oxygen cannula pumping life into her airway. He could see a droop on the left side of her face. She clearly couldn't speak as the conversation between her and her son was completely one-sided.

Prince Louis insisted, "You served this country superbly, but now in the interest of your health, I want you to sign this, Mummy."

James shook his head as he watched a woman barely able to hold a pen being coached on scribbling on a document with her son guiding her hand.

As she finished, Gardenia hugged his father. The delight between them sickened James.

Gardenia exclaimed, "I'm so proud of you, Your Majesty!"

James broke in and cheered, "Long live the queen!"

Louis turned, a nervous shock. "James, what a surprise."

James smiled. "I understand."

"Well, Mum has abdicated the throne."

James held his hands out wide. "Well, then I guess I should congratulate you and say 'Long live the king.'"

Louis relaxed. "Thank you, James."

James held a finger up. "One more thing, father." He pulled out the tape recorder. "I want you to hear something." He hit play.

From the tape, the queen's voice said, "Make it happen."

His father's voice responded, "Will the people accept another death?"

Richard's voice conceded, "The masses undoubtedly."

James breathed a lion's breath, hard and angry. He listened on.

The four of them listened. James could see the queen reliving the recording for the second time, her eyes rolling around as though an amusement ride had upset her stomach.

The queen continued. "James has forced this move. For the good of the country."

Louis insisted, "It must look like an accident."

The queen cackled, "With all due speed. But no more miscalculations. My love, you'll handle it personally."

Richard's voice beamed, "Yes, Your Majesty."

The tape recorder played out to the stunned and silent new king. James put it down on the bed. "You can have this tape. The original is in a safe place."

James tossed a document onto the bed. "That's for you."

Louis picked up the paper. "What's this?"

James gestured with his head. "You just gave one to Grandmother. Don't tell me you don't know what that is."

"Abdication? You expect me to abdicate after all the years I have sat and waited?" He grumbled, "After all the abuse I took from this ... thing?" He waved the paper at his own mother. "You can't be serious?"

James remained unmoved. "You have no choice, Your Majesty." He twisted the title like a knife.

"No way, no, no, no."

Gardenia, for her part, reasoned up the only available sanity. "Sign it, Louis."

Louis gathered his senses and shot back. "We underestimated you." He put the document against his mother's shoulder and signed with a push against the queen Mother. He came around the bed and tossed the document at James's feet. "Now you're king. Excellent coup. Just so you know, you are no different. I would feel proud of you except—"

Gardenia snapped, "Shut up, Louis."

"Well, you don't get it, Louis." For the first time in his life he called his father by his first name, distancing his relationship from a man he had no respect for. "I've found my queen, and the only kingdom I want is the one we will make together. You see, I plan on asking Alba to marry me. She's a Buddhist, so I'm leaving the church. As you know, that makes it impossible for me to become king."

"You're giving this up? But that means the throne ... Malcolm?"

James thought about his brother. Malcolm would make a great king, one who would reset the royal compass. "Yes. Long live the king."

Chapter 61

Five days passed, and while Malcolm prepared, James held many of the royal duties of kingship. The country waited for the passing of the crown to its rightful holder.

On a fall day, six years to day of his mother's death, the nation listened as a TV reporter announced, "Today the royal line of succession climaxes a week of astounding events. The accidental death of Prince Richard followed by the queen's debilitating stroke."

James watched as Woom pushed one of her boys, Malcolm, in his wheelchair down the aisle of St. William Cathedral. James could only smile. Beside him was a beleaguered Prince Louis, resigned to the fact he would never reign as king.

When Malcolm made it to James, James stepped in and waved Woom off. He pushed his brother the remainder of the way. Positioned in front of the scarlet-robed archbishop, who held the crown above the next king.

James patted Malcolm as the archbishop called out, "Malcolm Henry George Edward Arthur Spencer Merlin …"

Malcolm painfully twisted his torso to gaze up at James.

James nodded—brothers, rivals united and bonded forever as Christina's sons.

The archbishop continued. "I now crown you, King Malcolm the Tenth."

James whispered in his ear, "Congratulations, Your Majesty."

As the thunder of roars shook the cathedral, Alba slipped forward and worked herself beside James.

King Malcolm reached out and grabbed a hand of his brother and one of Alba's. He pulled them close and, against the din of noise, said, "As king, my first duty and proclamation is ..." he said to James, "Do you have the ring?"

James pulled out the ring his mother had been promised by Ali Hassan, a gift from Al Hassan.

Malcolm continued. "I pronounce you man and wife."

This caught Alba by surprise. "Can he do that?"

James laughed. "He's the king."

She glowed as James put the ring on her finger then said to Malcolm, "Thank you, Your Majesty." She bent forward and kissed him.

Malcolm grinned. "Is that what I had to do to get a kiss from you?"

James shook his brother's hand. "Take care of our country. I have my own destiny."

Malcolm nodded. "What will I do without you?"

"Don't worry. I'm leaving Colin and Woom behind."

Malcolm scanned the room. "What about Warden?"

"I have to keep some help."

James and Alba took each other's hand and backed away as the throng of adoring citizens worked their way to touch the king. It was the first time a king allowed himself to be the people's king.

The couple smiled and breathed in the crisp morning air as they stepped out of the cathedral doors. A bounce in the newlyweds' steps.

James turned to Alba and held up a passport.

Alba grinned and held up hers.

James kissed her and said, "Oh, I almost forgot." He dug into another pocket and pulled out two toothbrushes.

Alba laughed and kissed James again.

Behind them a new flag unfurled, three scallops. Christina's coat of arms had been raised again.

James checked the time. Next to his wristwatch, a snake tattoo. He turned to Alba. "Do you want children?"

"Of course."

"May I ask a favor?"

She nodded.

"If we have a daughter, could we name her Christina?"

Alba smiled.

Then James and Alba walked among the celebrating crowd filling the street, anonymously blending in like water into a river.

CPSIA information can be obtained
at www.ICGtesting.com
Printed in the USA
FSOW01n2222241115
13781FS

9 781480 823136